THE WONDER OF PAINTING DRAGONS

THE WONDER OF PAINTING DRAGONS

AUSTIN COLTON

For more information, contact: www.austincolton.com

Paperback ISBN: 979-8-90030-272-0

Printed in the United States of America

10 9 8 7 6 5 4 3 2 1

Dedicated to Shawn Hays.

Thank you for teaching me the magic of reading.
It has filled my life with a wonder that has shaped my imagination forever.

CONTENTS

I
THE FIRE

A red dragon with wings the size of buildings soared over the city. Ciaran froze, dropping his basket of eggs on the ground, completely mesmerized by the majestic creature. The way the red scales reflected the sunlight showed such a range of shades that he could hardly count them all. Ciaran's wonder was shattered as he was shoved from behind. Stumbling forward, he caught himself before he fell on his face. Glaring at the man who had run into him, Ciaran saw that the older man was not at all awestruck by the sudden appearance of the dragon. Instead, his eyes were filled with terror and his lips were pulled back into a grimace. Looking back at the sky, Ciaran saw that the dragon had circled around and was now facing him. The dragon's long neck was extended, showcasing a darker underbelly, the scales black from chin to tail.

He heard several screams, but he didn't look to see where they came from. Instead, he continued to watch in amazement, which was now tarnished by fear, as the dragon folded in its leathery wings and then dove towards the city. Just before it would have crashed into the temple, its wings extended once more and it seemed to stop. The dragon flew just above the roof of the Temple of Umris that sat on the highest hill of the city. Belching fire, the roof of the temple ignited, and then the dragon soared away. Ciaran watched it climb into the sky and then disappear from view.

Smoke rose from the center of the temple, billowing thick and black into a pristine blue sky. Ciaran ran down the street, joining the crowd of frantic people who were shouting in alarm. Many were rushing towards the fire, but those who were trying to flee added to the chaos all around. Struggling through the throng, Ciaran forced his way past a cart which was blocking the way and entered the main street that led from the city square to the edge of the temple grounds. Without buildings blocking his view, he could see the fire as it burned across the roof of the western wing of the temple. Several roof tiles had broken and flames flickered their destructive tongues in the sky.

Finding shelter beneath the fabric awning of a bakery, Ciaran watched as the flames continued to burn the temple. Thousands still gathered in the streets while hundreds more rushed up and down the temple steps, bringing buckets of water to try and douse the flames. Night fell and the flames continued to burn. The air stank of smoke.

Resting on the ground, Ciaran held his head in his hands, fighting back tears. He loved spending time inside the walls just so he could admire the paintings and tapestries within. Ciaran knew them well and he grit his teeth at the thought of them being destroyed. Hundreds of years of art from the greatest masters who'd ever lived was on display in Umris's Temple. It was likely now that they were all gone and that he would never get to see them again.

Ciaran remained where he was through the night, waiting until the fire went out. Just before dawn, the fire began to wane and then was snuffed out, like a blown out candle. The smoke disappeared, while the smell lingered in the air. Everyone was silent, and then the crowd began to disperse, people returning to their homes. Even Ciaran was tired and longed for his bed, he knew he would not be able to sleep until he saw it.

Walking to the temple, he trudged up the hundred pristine marble steps, his heart sinking with every passing moment. Reaching the top, he paused, and stared at the scorched marble columns. The dragon fire had melted part of the stone to a slag which had dripped down like the column was a candle. The roof tiles were scored black and the wooden joists beneath were severely burned, the cracked charcoal white in places.

Ciaran wasn't the only one who had gone up to the temple. He recognized several of the master artisans, their red clothing and long black capes marking them.

"What a travesty. Why did this happen?" one of them explained, motioning towards the door which had burned and fallen to the ground. "So much lost in a single day."

"Cursed dragon! Why would the Goddess allow such destruction?"

The master artisans noticed Ciaran, but didn't pay him much attention. Still, he felt compelled to slouch as he slunk past them and entered the temple. Inside, the priests and priestesses were moving about, frantically working to remove works of art which had been spared or had only been slightly damaged by the flames. Standing in the entrance, Ciaran felt his heart fall as he looked on the far wall which was now completely ruined. The greatest artwork of the city was gone, the paint and canvas completely burned away. The once pristine marble wall was now charred black with smoke stains that ran towards a roof which was no longer there. Through the holes, Ciaran could see the blue sky and the sun which was still rising in the distance. Beams of light streamed in, their brilliant glow contrasting the great destruction.

Ciaran didn't know what to think. He could barely understand the pain and sorrow that he felt. He was completely overwhelmed by the sorrow that had resulted in seeing the destruction. He forced himself not to cry. Ciaran was no longer a boy, and his jaw was clenched so tightly it hurt.

More and more people were crowding in behind him, which forced Ciaran to move further into the temple. He eventually ended up on the far side, almost pressed against the wall. Just as he was about to try and squirm through the crowd and find his way home, the loud murmur of voices went silent. Heads turned and through gaps in people, Ciaran could see a figure enter the temple.

A woman emerged, dressed in a white gown with the hem of her dress stained black from soot. The priestess strode through the crowd with ease, everyone parting for her. She stopped at the back wall, close to where Ciaran was standing which provided him a better view. The priestess placed her hand against the wall, and tears began to stream down her face. She didn't cry for long and as the crowd began to grow restless, she turned around and smiled through her sorrow.

"Do not despair," the priestess said. "Though we can never replace what is lost, we have the power to rebuild. I ask you all, is this city not filled with the greatest artisans in the world?"

There were grunts and calls of affirmation from many. Ciaran looked at the men and women dressed in red. Each one had a stoney expression, their chins raised.

"We can use the time to prepare," the priestess continued. "In three months, it will be time to celebrate the anniversary of Umrithos. When the great Goddess Umris graced our first ancestors with the gift of the arts, she blessed this land and this temple we have built as a monument to that great day. We shall honor her as never before. We shall have a contest where all shall be invited to present their craft and those who are deemed worthy, shall have their art displayed in the rebuilt temple and bring honor back to this great city."

The crowd broke into applause, but Ciaran was too

awestruck to join in. His heart leapt within him, an excitement and hope he had never before experienced. This was his chance, the opportunity he had always hoped for but never thought would arrive. Ciaran might just be able to apprentice himself to a master and could finally learn all he needed to become the painter he'd always dreamed of being. He would paint that dragon, so majestic and destructive. As this thought solidified in his heart, he knew it was right. Finally, he smiled and joined in with the applause.

Ciaran entered the front door of his house and found his mother in the kitchen kneading bread. Her hands and wrists were covered in flour and the light brown apron which hung from her neck was similarly dusted. Sunlight streamed in through the kitchen window, making his mothers' honey colored hair glow. He wished he had been born with lighter colored hair instead of dark muddy locks. Ciaran saw relief in her mothers eyes even though she gave him a stern expression.

"Where have you been, young man? I was worried sick." She threw down the bread and hurried over to the door. His mother gave him a big hug, holding him tight. She smelled of flour and he knew that his shirt would now be dusty.

"Sorry ma. I stayed out to watch the fire. I was so worried."

"Never stay out like that again."

"I won't, ma."

"I'm glad you are safe. Tell me, what happened?"

"Ma," Ciaran said, pulling out of the hug. "The dragon blew fire on the temple and it burned everything."

"Oh, how terrible. Was there nothing saved?"

"A few things, but the great works are all gone."

His mother gave him another hug. "I'm sorry my boy. I know how much you loved to see the masterpieces."

"I know. But, there is some good news. The priestess said there will be a competition at the anniversary celebrations and all may submit art. Ma, I might have a chance at becoming an artist. I am certain one of the old masters will need help."

"How wonderful an opportunity, my dear."

"Do you think pa will agree?"

"I am certain your father will be happy to let you go for a few months. The larger portion of the work will not be needed until the end of spring which will fall just after the celebrations."

Ciaran smiled, though he did have a sinking feeling in his heart. If his father expected him to come back to work after he was apprenticed, then that would completely ruin his plans. He realized that was getting ahead of himself. He'd have to get a master to take him in first. Ciaran decided he would have to deal with his father later and though it was hard, he forced himself to set aside his worry.

"Why don't you go and get yourself cleaned up. You are dirty and I won't have you looking like that during supper." His mother gave him a kiss on the cheek; something Ciaran felt too old for, and then he hurried off down the hall and out to the back courtyard.

Their land was small, but it was walled off which gave them privacy. The bricks were of the deepest red and mortared together with a master's touch. Ciaran saw artistry in the way the bricks had been carefully stacked together and in the way the walls blended seamlessly with his home. He looked at the three story building, the small rectangular windows framed by tan stones rather than brick, and smiled. He looked at his own window and though the sun glinted off the glass, he could still make out the shapes of the paintings that hung on his wall. Excited, he hurried to the well, drew some water, and quickly took it inside to the washroom.

He used one of the stronger soaps to clean himself. Though it was not the one that smelled the best, it did strip off the grime and dirt much faster. The water was cold, but he didn't want to bother with heating some over the fire. Ciaran's thoughts were of painting and dragons as he finished scooping the final ladle of water out of the bucket to rinse all remaining soap suds from his skin. He toweled off, changed into a clean yellow indoor tunic with matching stockings, then hurried up the rickety stairs to his bedroom.

Ciaran's bed was pushed into the corner to provide him with as much working space as possible. An easel, hand made by his father, sat in the corner, a fresh canvas sitting on it. His desk, which sat under the window, wasn't tidy, but every small glass bottle or clay pot had its place. Several freshly mixed paints were sitting out on a small block of green tunic. He felt a sense of longing to also wear that color and be recognized as an apprentice to one of the great artists. She raised an eyebrow at him and uncertain what to do, he bowed.

"Can I help you?" the girl asked.

"I am here to offer my services to Master Painter Hilde."

"She is not looking for any more help. We are busy, please go away."

Before Ciaran could get another word in, the door closed, the lock clicking into place.

At least she didn't slam it closed, he thought as he turned away.

It took a bit more effort to keep the smile on his face, but he persisted, and when he arrived at the next large brick building that was the art studio of the most famous artist in the city, he froze. Standing outside in his red clothing and black cape, was Lord Aidan. He was frowning as he cast an old painting down upon the ground. Catching only a glimpse, Ciaran was awestruck at the masterpiece of oil paint and almost called out as it landed picture side down on the dirty street. Lord Aidan stomped on the canvas and then spit on it. He reeled, his face full of fury and anger, then shouted at two younger boys in green tunics.

"Fetch me new canvas and paints. Now! Before I cast you out like that rubbish painting."

The artist apprentices sprinted away, their arms whirling as they hurried down to the markets. Lord Aidan turned, his eyes falling on Ciaran. The scowl on the mans face made

Ciaran take a step back in fear. Then, glancing at the street, he hurried on, not bothering to ask to apprentice for Lord Aidan.

Studio after studio turned Ciaran down. Though most were brusque, a few were kind and even one artist made a brief appearance to turn him down herself. She reminded him of his mother, with honey hair and a kind smile.

"My dear, I simply do not have the time to train you," the artist said. "Every artist in the city will be too busy to take you on and apprentice you. Time demands only our best."

"But I can paint," Ciaran protested. "Please, I can..."

"Dear, come back after the festival and I would be happy to see what you can do. Right now, I have all the help I need."

The woman smiled, patted him on the cheek, and went back inside. One of her apprentices lingered, another boy who was perhaps three or four years Ciaran's senior. His hair was trimmed so short that he almost looked bald. He had a bright smile, but there was a glint in his eye like he was amused. The apprentice reached out his hand, offering it to Ciaran. Shaking the older boy's hand, Ciaran felt his smile return.

"What is your name, boy?"

"Ciaran."

"It's a pleasure to meet you Ciaran. I'm Declan. Mistress Deirdre is a good teacher, but she is right."

"I know," Ciaran said, his heart sinking.

"But there is a man who just might take you in."

green tunic. He felt a sense of longing to also wear that color and be recognized as an apprentice to one of the great artists. She raised an eyebrow at him and uncertain what to do, he bowed.

"Can I help you?" the girl asked.

"I am here to offer my services to Master Painter Hilde."

"She is not looking for any more help. We are busy, please go away."

Before Ciaran could get another word in, the door closed, the lock clicking into place.

At least she didn't slam it closed, he thought as he turned away.

It took a bit more effort to keep the smile on his face, but he persisted, and when he arrived at the next large brick building that was the art studio of the most famous artist in the city, he froze. Standing outside in his red clothing and black cape, was Lord Aidan. He was frowning as he cast an old painting down upon the ground. Catching only a glimpse, Ciaran was awestruck at the masterpiece of oil paint and almost called out as it landed picture side down on the dirty street. Lord Aidan stomped on the canvas and then spit on it. He reeled, his face full of fury and anger, then shouted at two younger boys in green tunics.

"Fetch me new canvas and paints. Now! Before I cast you out like that rubbish painting."

The artist apprentices sprinted away, their arms whirling as they hurried down to the markets. Lord Aidan turned, his eyes falling on Ciaran. The scowl on the mans face made

Ciaran take a step back in fear. Then, glancing at the street, he hurried on, not bothering to ask to apprentice for Lord Aidan.

Studio after studio turned Ciaran down. Though most were brusque, a few were kind and even one artist made a brief appearance to turn him down herself. She reminded him of his mother, with honey hair and a kind smile.

"My dear, I simply do not have the time to train you," the artist said. "Every artist in the city will be too busy to take you on and apprentice you. Time demands only our best."

"But I can paint," Ciaran protested. "Please, I can..."

"Dear, come back after the festival and I would be happy to see what you can do. Right now, I have all the help I need."

The woman smiled, patted him on the cheek, and went back inside. One of her apprentices lingered, another boy who was perhaps three or four years Ciaran's senior. His hair was trimmed so short that he almost looked bald. He had a bright smile, but there was a glint in his eye like he was amused. The apprentice reached out his hand, offering it to Ciaran. Shaking the older boy's hand, Ciaran felt his smile return.

"What is your name, boy?"

"Ciaran."

"It's a pleasure to meet you Ciaran. I'm Declan. Mistress Deirdre is a good teacher, but she is right."

"I know," Ciaran said, his heart sinking.

"But there is a man who just might take you in."

firewood where Ciaran was patiently waiting for them to dry. He wanted to see how the colors looked when they weren't wet. No matter how hard he tried, his mixtures never seemed to hold their strong hues after the drying process, which was agonisingly long.

Laying down on his bed, Ciaran looked at the paintings which hung from the walls. Many were of nature, a poor representation of the hills and mountains north of the city, and one deeply flawed depiction of the temple before it had burned. He didn't understand what was wrong with it. The paint and the detail were thin and hardly a brushstroke could be seen. But the shapes didn't come together and it didn't quite look real. His parents hadn't been of any help, telling him it was a great painting. It irritated Ciaran that they did that. To them, everything he did was great. Only Maeve was honest with him. She had told him that it was no good. He'd appreciated her honesty.

Though he was tired, not having slept a wink the night before because of the fire, Ciaran got out of his bed and left his room. He hurried downstairs and saw his mother was laying out the bread dough on the baking stones.

"Where are you off too in such a hurry?"

"I was going to see Maeve before supper."

"Alright, but make sure you are home soon."

"Of course ma, I won't be too long."

"You are welcome to invite Maeve over for supper."

"I will."

Waving his goodbye, Ciaran left his home and was surprised at how busy his street was. Every single one of his neighbors seemed to be gathered outside, talking with one another. He spotted his father arguing with several other men on the corner. Ducking his head so he wouldn't be spotted, Ciaran started down the road opposite where his father was. The home at the end of the street was small, only two stories, but its walls encircled a much larger section of land. He could smell the flowers of the blooming orchard, the sweet scents joining in with the dusty hay smell of the street.

Maeve was sweeping the steps in front of her home. Her red hair glimmered in the sunlight and her freckles seemed to shine in the afternoon light. Ciaran was about to run, but he wasn't a boy any longer, so he forced himself to keep the same pace. His friend smiled when she noticed him and Ciaran smiled back.

"Hail and well met, Maeve!" Ciaran called.

Setting her broom against the door, she leapt down from the steps and hurried to meet him. "Hail and well met, Ciaran."

"Did you hear the news?"

"I did. So, are you going to do it?" Maeve asked.

"I am going to try," Ciaran said. "If I could help a master painter, I might be able to learn what I need. Finally become accepted. I don't want to make bricks for the rest of my life. Not like pa."

"Papa said that all the artisans are looking for more apprentices. I am certain you will find someone who will take you in."

"I hope so."

Maeve giggled with excitement. "If they do accept you, what are you going to paint?

"I am going to paint a dragon."

"Are you certain that is a good idea? I mean, this whole mess is the fault of a dragon."

"I just feel like it makes sense to paint the mighty creature, even if it is responsible for destroying the temple and the art."

"Or do you want to paint it to honor it for giving you the chance to become an artist?"

"Perhaps a bit of both."

"I can't wait to see your painting."

"Are you going to try and do something as well?" Ciaran asked.

"Papa and I are going to make some baskets, but not for the competition."

"Ma said you could come to dinner if you want."

"That would be lovely. Papa will be out so I was going to eat on my own." Maeve looked at her broom, then nodded. "Let me just get this finished and we can go."

"Great. What can I do to help?"

2
THE OLD MASTER

Stunned, Ciaran stared for a moment at the door that had just been slammed in his face. The master artisan had simply looked at him and before he could speak a word, dismissed him. As the shock wore off, Ciaran straightened his posture, and made his way down the street to the next large brick building. He forced himself to take a deep breath as he walked up to the second door. Ciaran knocked firmly upon the door. The sound as his knuckles struck the wood wasn't as loud as he expected, the wood thick and heavy. Glancing at the brass door knocker, Ciaran used that as well. The resounding three thumps were much louder. Taking a step back, he clasped his hands before him, ready with his best smile.

When the door opened, a girl a few years older than Ciaran looked out. She was dressed in the green tunic of an apprentice and she had a bit of white paint on her cheek. Ciaran was immediately struck in awe of the girl and the stay. With every passing moment, his heart began pounding in his chest and he started breathing faster. He heard something scrape against the inside of the door and then it was pulled open. The scent of oil paint and turpentine was strong, as was the stench of old cabbage and radish.

"What do you want?" an old cranky voice said as the door opened further.

The old master's eyes were deep set and surrounded by wrinkles. A pair of spectacles sat half way down his long hooked nose. His snarl showed yellow teeth that had gaps between them. Ciaran resisted the urge to take a step away from the man as the scent of radish and cabbage grew stronger. Instead, he bowed deeply and held his hands behind his back.

"Forgive the intrusion. I was told that you were seeking an apprentice to help with your painting for the Goddess."

"How did you come by this information?"

"I was told that you had mentioned you needed help to the baker," Ciaran said, gesturing. He kept his head bowed, afraid to look up at the master. He also didn't want to mention Declan or any other artist, just in case that would cause harm to his chances of being accepted.

The old master grumbled then let the door swing all the way open. "No sense turning away help when it comes to your doorstep. Come on in, boy. Let's see if you will be up to the task. If you are worth the effort, I suppose having a spry boy around to fetch things for me would be worthwhile. These knees are not as limber as they once were."

Ciaran's heart leapt in his chest and he had to force

himself not to smile. Entering the small studio, he closed the door behind him. The smells of paint were strong and the hallway which led deeper into the building wasn't well lit. There was a staircase to his right and doors to the left. The old man had already walked to the end of the hall and past a curtain which hung down to cover an archway. Hurrying after him, Ciaran pushed past the curtain and was almost blinded by the brightness of the room beyond. The ceiling was domed and there was a large hole in the center which let in a great deal of sunlight. He could see a strange contraption that held up a circular slab of wood which could be closed by pulling on a rope. The room had many windows on the far wall allowing in more light.

Tables filled the large space and every single one of them was covered with strange instruments, paint brushes, bottles, and easels. Half finished paintings, clay or stone sculptures, and charcoal drawings on parchment were scattered about. It was a brilliant mess and Ciaran was both amazed and overwhelmed by it all.

The old master waved him over as he took a seat on a stool. A large canvas had been set up which was already covered in red and brown paint. The smears looked like they had been slathered across the canvas with a large brush. Beside the old man was a small table with a rather elaborate assortment of paints, brushes, and cleaning jars. A painter's palate was set on the edge, with several dark shades of brown or red already mixed together. As Ciaran looked at the paints, he wondered if there would be enough to cover such an enormous canvas.

Without thinking, he pointed to the canvas and asked a question. "What are you painting?"

"That is for me to know and everyone else to find out."

"I apologize," Ciaran said, bowing again. "I shouldn't have asked."

The old man chuckled. "Grab that stool over there boy and have a seat. I have a few questions for you."

Seeing a stool at a nearby table, Ciaran retrieved it and then took a seat an arms length away from the old master.

"What's your name?"

"Ciaran."

"Well, Ciaran, I am Edgar. Have you ever heard of me?"

"Yes. You painted one of the temple murals. Sadly, I think they were destroyed yesterday in the fire."

"Glad to hear that my name is still known to some." Edgar smiled. "Did you know who I was before you came here?"

"No."

"Then why did you come to my home instead of going to one of the other art studios or masters?"

Ciaran paused and shrugged, uncertain how to answer.

"Be honest with me boy, or you can leave now."

"I did go to the other studios. No one else seemed interested enough to take me on."

"Why do you want to be an art apprentice?"

"I want to learn how to paint."

"Of course. But why do you want to be an artist?"

"I see so much beauty in the world. I would like to be able to capture it and add to it if I can."

"The world has enough beautiful things already. Do you truly think it needs what you can make for it?"

"I am not making it for them," Ciaran answered. "I am making it for myself."

"If that is true, why do you seek a master? Can you not already paint? Should you not just continue as you are?"

Ciaran frowned, uncertain how to answer these questions to properly explain what he meant. The old master was smiling at him. It wasn't a kind smile, and it reminded him of the look a fox would have stalking a chicken. Ciaran forced himself to stand up tall and raise his chin.

"Should I not demand the very best from myself?" Ciaran asked, his voice a bit more defiant than he had intended. "How is the making of art any different than other work? If I wanted to till the ground and grow corn to feed myself, should I not learn the best way? Would it not be wise for me to use the best tools to produce the best crop? My father makes bricks and has taught me that the best bricks come from the best clay. He has instructed me on mixing bricks from quality materials, taking care not to rush my work. If I wanted to make bricks for my own house, I would make them from the best materials. I would take my time just as I would be careful and deliberate raising the crops for my food. Is that really any different than how one should approach art? I say no. "

Edgar frowned, then got to his feet. "Interesting argument. I see the point you are trying to make. Remember, art is about both things; making it for yourself as well as sharing it with others. It is not an easy balance and one many artisans fail to understand. But you are right in perhaps the most important thing. You must demand the very best from yourself, anything less is a waste. Are you truly dedicated enough to put in the work required to become such an artist?"

"I am."

"Good. Can you write?"

"I can."

"Very well. Now tell me, Ciaran, do you already have talent with a brush?"

"A bit. Really, all I can do is mix paints and colors. I don't have much skill or instruction with the brush." Ciaran wasn't sure how much to tell and decided he would be open and honest. "My paintings lack true form as well. Sometimes the details appear correct, but the overall composition isn't right. My backgrounds do not complement the foreground, or some things do not appear in correct proportions."

"All common problems. Things which can be learned over time through practice and careful observation." Edgar motioned to his painting. "Patience and deliberate action are keys as well. As you can see, I am preparing my painting with an underpainting. Do you know why?"

"No."

"When you build a home with bricks, do you just start laying down bricks without a plan?"

"Of course not?"

"What do you do?"

"A true builder will carefully design the building, using

basic arithmetic to number the needed bricks and plot out the space to lay a foundation. Only once everything is prepared, will they begin to set down the first brick."

"What I am doing is very similar. Planning out and preparing my canvas for what I want to paint. If you wish to become a good artist, the best place to start is by learning to observe. Do you have paper?"

"I only brought a small piece with me."

Ciaran reached into his pocket to retrieve his paper, but Master Edgar shook his head.

"See that table in the corner? Go and retrieve an empty book. There should be more than one, so you may choose whichever you like. There should also be new silverpoint pencils. Great for sketching and writing since they do not require ink."

Ciaran obeyed, and went to the table in the corner. It, like every other table, was cluttered and seemed messy, but there was some level of organization to the chaos. Used notebooks with drawings and writings were piled up on the right. Newer notebooks were piled on the left, and the middle of the table was filled with small wooden boxes. Opening a box, Ciaran saw long sticks of charcoal wrapped in cloth. Closing it, he opened another and found several wooden rods inside. A small tip of silver glued to the wood with a hard black enamel. Removing one of the silverpoint pencils, he shut the box, then looked at the stacks of empty books. Their covers were soft leather, with a flap to cover the edges of the reddish paper, and a long cord which wrapped around the book several times. Most of the books were of the same design, the biggest difference being the size and color of the pages. Some had paper that was more reddish brown, like the paint Edgar had applied to the canvas, while others were more cream colored, perhaps even yellow. Ciaran took a moment to examine a book of each color paper, deciding he would go with a darker color. Then, he went for a medium size book. It was comfortable in his hand, so it wouldn't be difficult to carry, but the pages were still large enough that he would have room to draw and write.

He held his new book and pencil with reverence as he walked back to the old master. Ciaran knew that what he had just been given was worth perhaps two weeks wages for his father; perhaps more. Taking a seat on the stool, he looked up at the master who was swirling his brush in a thin dark brown paint.

"Good, you have chosen a notebook."

"Thank you."

"My boy, what is wrong? You look distressed."

Ciaran held up the book. "This is simply a costly gift."

"Bah! Nonsense. Those books were donated to me long ago. I will not live long enough to use them all. More books can be made, Ciaran. Do not be afraid to use it simply because it has great cost. When I was a much younger artist, I worried that I must learn first by using cheap materials. But learning is always an expense. So I decided not to waste time and effort on lesser things."

"Yes, of course. Thank you."

Edgar turned to his canvas and began to apply the brown paint. "Are you ready to get to work?"

"Yes. What would you have me do?"

"I need you to go and get me more paint. I want you to write my instructions down in your book."

Ciaran unwrapped the chord, opened his book, and prepared himself to write.

"I do not purchase paints from the markets. There are many others who do, but the best materials should be made by hand. I need six colors. White, yellow, blue, red, green, and brown. Now pay attention. I need specific pigments to mix the correct value."

The old master began to describe in exact detail where Ciaran needed to go to get the pigments. He wrote down the instructions on the first two pages of his new book. The silverpoint pencil made clear markings on the dark paper. When he was done, the master had him read back the instructions. Ciaran did and received a nod of approval from his new master.

"Now go. It will take you a few days to travel to where the materials are. Do not feel rushed in attaining them. I will prepare for you to return with quality pigments, understand?"

"Yes, I understand."

"Good. When you return, I will teach you how to grind the pigments to powder, and to mix them into paint."

"Of course, Master Edgar."

"There is one more thing you need before you go."

Edgar set down his brush, then groaned as he got to his

feet. The old man walked to another table set under the large windows of the back wall. Ciaran followed him, clutching his notebook tightly. Edgar picked up a large leather bag that had a single strap, then handed it to Ciaran.

"Everything you need for harvesting the pigments should be inside. Make sure to get enough to fill each jar."

"I will."

"And make sure no one follows you. I have spent a long time searching for the best ingredients to make my paint. If word got out, then these spots would be ruined and I would have to start over. Do you understand?

"Yes. I understand, Master Edgar."

"Good. Now go, I must get back to work."

Ciaran bowed to the master who hobbled back to his stool. Watching the master pick up the brush, Ciaran delayed a moment to watch as Edgar began to add dark brown paint to the canvas. It was added in splotches which did not make sense. Ciaran wondered what his master was painting. Not wanting to get yelled at, he forced himself to leave, regretting that he wouldn't be able to sit and watch the master work. But Ciaran was still excited and there was a skip to his step as he pulled back the curtain and entered the dark hallway. He had found a master to teach him, and Ciaran was determined to make the most from this new opportunity.

3
THE ART GOBLIN

Ciaran finished placing the seed cakes, dried meat, and wax dipped cheese into his pack, making sure it wouldn't move around. Satisfied that he had enough food for a week's worth of exploring, he pulled the draw string tight and slung it over his shoulder. He felt a little awkward, standing in the kitchen with a travel pack on his back and the artist's bag hanging from his side. Ciaran felt like he was going to tip over. He looked at his mother, who was standing by the door. She was holding a walking stick.

"Here, take this. It should help to make traveling easier on you."

"Thanks, ma," Ciaran said as he took the walking stick.

"Now, promise me that you will be safe?"

"I promise that I will be. I won't be going far. Everything I need should be in the surrounding hills. It's just going to take a bit of wandering about to find exactly what I am looking for."

"Just, be careful. I don't like the idea of you going alone. Are you certain that no one will go with you?"

"Ma, I already told you. Master Edgar doesn't want his secret to get out. I have to go find everything alone."

Ciaran's mother smiled, gave him a hug, and wished him well as he left. Although Ciaran wished he could say goodbye to his father, he didn't want to bother him. It was past midday and they would be preparing the kilns for brick firing. It didn't seem like a good idea to go in and distract his father for just a simple goodbye.

The streets of Umrithos were filled with chatter as people bustled about. There was a sense of urgency in the air and people walked faster than normal. It seemed strange to Ciaran that so many would be in a rush, seeing as how few of them would be making art. But then, as he rounded the corner of a street which provided him with a better view of the temple, he was reminded how much damage the fire had caused.

What had always stood as a beautiful white monument at the top of the hill was now black like the wick of a snuffed out candle. It would take more than just art to repair the building and he could see a line of carts filled with cut logs making their way down the temple road. He didn't doubt that by the time he returned to the city, many would be hard at work replacing the burned roofing and polishing the scorched stone.

He walked through the streets unbothered, managing a slow but steady pace through the crowds of the market as he made his way towards the gate. The main road, which lead from the temple to the gate, was by far the largest and busiest of the city. Hundreds of horse-drawn carts, carriages, and waggons went past him, congesting the road. People weaved their way between them when needed, but mostly stayed to either side. The buildings that lined either side of the road were mostly shops, the living quarters in the second or third stories above. Many buildings' second stories hung over the first floor, which provided an overhang where many had attached ropes or hooks to display additional goods in front of their open doors. Between buildings or down adjacent streets, the vendors set up tables or booths, some with tarps hanging over them to provide shade from the sun and a small measure of relief from the heat of the day.

Ciaran wondered why they bothered, seeing sweat drip from a merchant's face. One merchant had a thick mustache and he was selling all manner of tools. As the man called out to everyone who passed by, boasting of his wares, Ciaran was surprised to find himself tempted. Among the tools was a paint brush that had an enamel handle that was painted blue. The hair on the end of the brush was fine and pointed. He had three coins in a small purse attached to his belt, but he knew the purchase wasn't worth it. Ciaran ducked his head and continued on his way, wondering why he was so drawn to the paint brush. Master Edgar would have plenty, but he still felt a strange longing inside. He managed to force his mind away from the paint brush, telling himself that if he still had his money when he returned, he would buy it. Instead of making him feel better, Ciaran only felt worried that he wouldn't find the paint brush again. Grumbling, he looked over his shoulder, hoping to catch a glimpse of the vendor, but he had passed out of view.

It took him another hour to walk down the rest of the street. Ciaran joined the long line of people waiting to pass out of the gate. The arched exit of the city was guarded by five soldiers on either side. Two large towers sat on either side of the gate and the wooden door was held up by chains which were attached to pulleys on each tower. Ciaran traced the chains, observing where they disappeared into the tower walls. He found the system interesting and wondered how much effort it took to raise the gate. His curiosity soon shifted from the gate to the guards who were standing at the ready. New machines had been set out on the towers that looked like large bows mounted on a horizontal wheel. The arrows, which were notched and ready, looked more like spears and the tips were made from a clear stone.

Diamonds? Ciaran wondered, noticing how they sparkled so brightly in the sunlight. The sheer value of such a large diamond being used as a spear sized arrowhead was difficult for Ciaran to imagine. *Who could afford such an expense?*

He was certain that the new weapons had been set out in case the red dragon returned. As the thought entered his mind, Ciaran found himself looking up at the sky, half afraid, half hopeful. There was no dragon to be seen and the thin wisps of clouds rippled across the sky. The sun was beginning its descent towards the horizon and he was beginning to feel hot with his pack and artist's bag. Wiping a bit of sweat from his brow, Ciaran turned his attention back to the road and the group of farmers who were ahead of him in line.

When he reached the city gate, the guards waved him through without stopping him or asking questions. Ciaran gave them a polite nod, then hurried through the open gate. He kept his distance from the farmers on the road ahead, remaining at least a dozen steps back. The men were dirty from plowing the fields and smelled of the earth. As they followed the winding road to the south, the farmers began to depart, one by one, until they had all returned to their fields. Ciaran wasn't alone on the road, but the more fields he passed, the fewer carts rolled past him. When he reached the end of the paved section of road, where stones turned to dirt, he took a moment to pause. The road split and went in three directions. One would take him to the western mountains where he could begin his search for several of the ingredients. The road directly ahead would lead him to the lake, which was another important location. And the left road would take him down into the marshes, which was the final place to gather the pigments for the brown and green paints Master Edgar had requested. After a moment's deliberation, Ciaran decided to go right. He would start at the mountain and go in a circle. It seemed to him the best choice as the hike up to the mountain would be the most work.

"Best to get that out of the way first," he mumbled to himself as he adjusted his pack and started walking again.

The walking stick made satisfying thumps as it struck the dirt. It wasn't much, but it kept him from growing too bored during his walk. Ciaran took his first break to rest after another hour of walking. The back of his shirt was damp from sweat caused by the heat and the pack. Setting it down on the ground, he found a sizable boulder just to the side of the road and had a seat. He took a drink of water from his waterskin, and poured a small amount on the top of his head. It was cool and sent a shiver through his back as it trickled down his neck. Smiling, Ciaran began to tap his walking stick on the ground. The eagerness and urgency he had been feeling earlier had already faded and to occupy his mind, he began to think about painting.

He could picture the red dragon flying across the bright blue sky, the scales depicted in extreme detail. Ciaran envisioned himself laying down the paint with small brushstrokes, easily blending the colors together, working the oil paint to absolute perfection. Though he doubted he was capable of bringing his vision to life, he couldn't help but dream it up anyway. The more he thought, the more he felt he would be capable of this. Removing the leatherbound sketchbook from his pack, he turned to the first page, glanced at his instructions, then flipped the page. Staring at the dark red paper, he took the silverpoint pencil and began to sketch out what he pictured in his mind.

After a few minutes, he had the basic shapes of the dragon, two wings, serpent-like body, with front legs tucked close to the body while the back legs were stretched out. Still, his sketch was missing detail. Ciaran gripped his pencil tight, a little frustrated that he could see the dragon so clearly in his mind, but as soon as he opened his eyes to draw it, the blankness of the page seemed to overwhelm the picture. Making small lines, he attempted to scribble in some details, managing to make the sketch look even worse. Huffing, he began drawing on the next page, this time choosing a nearby tree as his point of reference. This sketch was easy and the pencil seemed to glide effortlessly on the paper. It didn't seem to take long before a tree, full of life and detail, was etched onto the page. Ciaran tapped the bottom of the silverpoint pencil against the page, perplexed. He was irritated at how easily he could draw from a reference, how he could hold a picture of the tree in his head, and draw it.

Why can't I do the same with the dragon?

His thinking was interrupted by a strange squealing sound. The underbrush and grass on the opposite side of the road began to shift as something moved through it. Leaping to his feet, Ciaran grabbed his walking stick and held it at the ready. The high pitched squeal returned, followed by what sounded like words.

"Help! Help!" the small voice cried.

A moment later, something emerged from the grass and leapt onto the road. The green creature was small as an acorn and it bounded across the path like a toad. It had large beady eyes that were a solid black. Both ears, half as large as its head, were pointed towards the sky. The tips of each ear were covered in small white hairs that glinted in the sunlight. A serpent slithered after the creature who was yelping and zig-zagging in an effort to avoid being captured.

"Help!" the small voice squeaked. "Please, help me!"

Ciaran reacted in an instant, sweeping the serpent aside with his walking stick. The snake hissed, then lashed out, trying to bite at Ciaran's ankles with long fangs. Leaping back, he avoided the snake and stabbed down with his stick. The bottom struck the serpent's side, making a hole in the scaled skin. Pulling up his stick, he struck again, this time hitting the snake in the head. It went limp and a little trickle of blood emerged from the snake's mouth. Ciaran prodded it, then used his walking stick to move the snake to the side of the road. Once it was hidden in the grass, he took a breath, then looked for the strange little creature that had called for his help.

Crouching in the middle of the hard dirt road, the little creature was looking up at Ciaran, his black eyes unblinking. Unsure what to make of the creature, Ciaran crouched down to get a better look. The small arms were folded, the hands having only three fingers tipped with small black claws. It wore a small brown shirt that was buttoned, and small trousers that were cut off just past the knees. The legs were shaped so they bent backwards, similar to a frog but the skin was more reptilian, like a lizard.

"What are you?" he asked the creature.

"I am Zict, the goblin. And you?"

Ciaran paused, then with a chuckle, answered. "I am Ciaran, the human. I have never met a goblin before. It's a pleasure to meet you."

"The pleasure is mine dear human! I must say, thank you for helping me. Those pesky snakes, always trying to make a meal out of me. And not a good meal either. I can't say I would taste all that good. A bit too stringy, or that's what grandmother always said."

Zict had an odd way of speaking, his large mouth moving more than it needed to. He was expressive, both with his face and with his hands. The goblin spoke with his entire body.

"I'm glad I could help. I must be going now."

"Going? So soon? No, I can not let you. Not until I have been able to properly thank you for your help."

"You have already thanked me. I really must be going."

Ciaran stepped around Zict, then started on his way. He heard the soft pitter patter of tiny feet behind him. The goblin was small, but it moved fast, keeping pace with him.

"Where are you going?" Zict asked.

"Into the mountains. I am searching for a small beetle that lives in the bark of red oak trees. I need to harvest their shells to make pigment for a paint."

"You are making paint?"

"Well, right now I am just getting the materials."

"Why didn't you say so?" Zict proclaimed, leaping nearly to Ciaran's eyes. The creature landed on his shoulder. He was light and the small claws on the edges of his three toes dug into Ciaran's tunic, holding the goblin in place. "See, I am an art goblin. We are small, simple folk, you see."

"An art goblin?" Ciaran asked, incredulous.

"Yes, an art goblin."

"What does a goblin know about art?"

"Much more than you. Tell me, how old are you, human?"

"Fourteen."

"Well, I'm two hundred and eighty. I am certain I know more about art than you ever will. Big humans, with short lives always, always think they know everything."

Zict did have a point, so Ciaran decided he wouldn't argue any further. "Since you are an art goblin, perhaps you could help me."

"Gladly. I owe you my life. Anything I can do to help repay this debt, I shall do. How may I be of assistance?"

"As I said, I am gathering materials to make paint. I have a list of what I need, and a general idea of where to go. But it might take me a long time to find everything. If you could help me find what I am looking for, then I shall consider your debt paid in full."

"This is an easy task. Zict will be happy to help. Let me see your list human!"

"Call me Ciaran."

"Of course, Ciaran."

Reaching down into his artist's satchel, Ciaran removed his sketch book. He opened the book to the first page where he had written all of Master Edgar's instructions. Zict moved from his shoulder, down his arm, the small claws pinching a bit as they clung to Ciaran's skin. The goblin hummed as he read the paper and Ciaran was intrigued that the goblin could read. He knew so little about the creature and was still doubtful that it was an expert in art.

"This will not do," Zict said, "this will not do at all!"

"What won't do?"

"These are not right. There are better places to go to find pigments to make paint. I can't let you go and get these. No, we must travel and get the best pigments. You humans are so foolish. Making red from beetle shells. No, the best place to get what you want is to visit the Ashroot Dryad of the Ember Grove."

"Where is that?"

"Just on the other side of that mountain. It's not too far. Well, not for you. It would take me ages to get there on my little legs. But you could get there in a week."

"I don't have that much time. Even if I did, I only have food for a couple of days."

"Food will not be a problem. This I can show you too. I never need to bring food with me. It is so easy to find when you know what to look for."

"But I really don't have that much time."

"Ciaran, if you can't find time for this, how do you expect to find time to make the best art?"

Ciaran paused, considering. "What about the other colors?"

"I can help you find them all," Zict said, leaping back onto Ciaran's shoulder. "Trust me, no other artist will ever have colors so pure or vibrant as those I shall help you find."

"And it will only take me a week?"

"Only a week. And then we will come back. I promise."

"Fine. I'll go where you lead. Where do we go first?"

"Let's make our way to the woods."

4

THE FORBIDDEN WILDERNESS

The sun was low in the sky when Ciaran arrived at the edge of the wood. Zict still clung to his shoulder and had been chattering endlessly since they started their walk. Though he might have grown weary at such persistent speaking while at home, he found the company in the wild to be a welcome relief from the loneliness and boredom he'd experienced during the first part of the day. But as they drew near to the large wall of trees, the goblin went quiet. Ciaran stopped and examined one of the enormous pines. The trunk was so thick that he could stretch out both arms and still, the trunk would be wider. It seemed to loom over him, the trunk bare of branches for several hundred feet before they sprang out near the top. The needles looked like little clumps, forming bulbous and spiky shapes close to the tips of the tree branches. None of the branches extended far, and though there were so many of the great trees growing close together, plenty of light still streamed through.

Stepping closer, Ciaran placed his hand against the large sections of twisting bark. It was hard to the touch, like a stone, but the texture was like any other tree. A rich scent emerged from the forest, a mixture of mulch and sweet pine. He had grown up hearing tales about this forest, and they always warned against entering. People who went into this forest had a tendency to get lost and never return. It had only taken a day, but he was now on the edge of the land of Umrir and the start of the wild lands. Ciaran felt the hairs on the back of his neck prickle and he looked down at his shoulder to the silent Zict who was still clinging to him.

"I am not so sure about this," Ciaran said, his voice quivering.

"It will take far too much time to go around. Through the woods is the only way."

"People say those who wander here never find their way out again."

"Most don't have a goblin to guide them through," Zict said, his small voice confident.

"Are you certain we won't get lost?"

"You can put your trust in me, Ciaran. We won't get lost."

"Well, I've come this far. No sense getting frightened and turning back now," Ciaran said, more to himself than to his new friend.

He strode past the first tree, then the second, and continued until he was surrounded. When he looked back over his shoulders, he realized that he could no longer see the way out. He was committed to his course, and though he did feel a small twinge of fear, Ciaran kept placing one foot in front of the other.

"Zict, are we going to make it to the other side before nightfall?"

"No. But there is a great place where we can camp and rest for the night. Safe and warm. They will watch over us."

"Who will watch over us?"

"You will see. They are nice and you will enjoy meeting them."

"Why won't you tell me?"

"I don't want to ruin the surprise."

"I don't need any surprises."

"Sure you do. Every artist needs to be surprised from time to time. Inspiration is derived from such moments, when ideas come to the mind in unexpected ways. If you want to be an artist, Ciaran, you are going to need to get used to being surprised. The better you get at it, the more often you will find it happening to you."

Once again, Ciaran found it hard to argue with the creature.

He was still torn between deciding if he thought Zict was telling him the truth, or just saying the things he wanted to hear. Ciaran didn't have much of a reason to trust or distrust the goblin, so he decided to trust him once more, pushing his doubts to the side. Should Zict prove himself untrustworthy, he could just as easily ignore him and go back to his original plan. Though, as he looked at the woods, he did wonder if he would be able to find his way out again all on his own.

Late afternoon turned into evening and the sunlight created a glow on the tops of the trees that made the leaves look like they were shining. The forest floor was growing dim, but Ciaran could still see his way forward. Unlike the walk to the forest, Zict didn't speak. Instead, the small goblin hummed or purred, the soft vibrations a constant drumming on his shoulder. Every time Ciaran looked down at Zict, he saw that the goblins' ears were twitching and his head was on a swivel. Ciaran mimicked the goblin, scanning the trees from side to side.

"What are you looking for?" Ciaran asked.

"I'm not looking as much as I am listening."

"What are you listening for then?"

"Singing. You will hear it and when we do, we know we are getting close."

They walked on and within twenty minutes soft music could be heard through the trees. At first, it seemed to Ciaran to be tinkling chimes on the wind. Then, the soft sounds of flutes and lyres and harps joined in with the chimes. It was a soft, simple melody that Ciaran had never heard before. Still, there was a familiarity to the music, like it was an old lullaby he had forgotten and was getting to re-experience for the first time.

"Go right at that big tree up ahead," Zict said, pointing with his tiny hand.

Ciaran obeyed, turning just before reaching one of the largest trees he'd ever seen. As he passed, he looked up at the behemoth, and thought he saw a face in the bark smiling down at him. The large branches near the top almost looked like an arm, the leaves at the end forming a hand to point the way. Shaking his head and closing his eyes, Ciaran looked again but did not see the face again. It was just a tree.

It is just a tree, he thought to himself, repeating it several times over.

The music became more distinct as they drew closer, but its volume remained quiet. It didn't seem to disturb the natural sounds of the forest. The humming of the insects, the chirping of the birds, and the rustle of leaves as they were caressed by the wind all seemed to melt together. The music complementing the natural sounds like a fine glaze on a well crafted piece of pottery. Though both were beautiful on their own, they became whole as they were placed together. It was this thought which finally put Ciaran's fear and apprehension to rest. As a deep breath escaped him, his shoulders relaxed and the tightness in his stomach faded. Completely and truly at ease, he walked past another tree and abruptly found himself in a meadow.

Flowers of all kinds were in bloom. The light from the setting sun made them shine brightly. Bell shaped flowers hung from thick green stalks, bees fluttering from flower to flower. Their buzz added to the music. Everything smelled so sweet, better than honey and richer than cream. Ciaran looked to his right and across the meadow, he saw a pond. Water flowed from a stream, falling over a small cliff into the clear water. Sitting on the edge were people. Or, at least, they looked like people.

The strange fold sat atop the cliff beside the waterfall. There were at least a dozen men and women playing instruments. Ciaran could see the harps and lyres on the right side, sitting in rows. On the left were the flute and chime players. Everyone was smiling, their eyes partially closed, completely lost in the music they were playing. Beside the pond, a dozen women in flowing green or yellow gowns were dancing with shaggy haired men in bright blue or orange vests. They danced in circles and as Ciaran watched, he noticed that the men were not wearing trousers, but that their legs were covered in dark fur, with hooves instead of feet. Ciaran smiled to himself.

"They are satyrs," he said, looking down at Zict who, to his surprise, was hugging a large bumble bee.

"Of course. Let's go speak with them. We don't have much longer. The festivities will end at twilight."

Not needing any extra encouragement, Ciaran strode through the meadow, completely at ease as he walked through the flowers. His fear of bees was also gone and he almost laughed as the small fuzzy insects landed on his trousers or tunic. Many made their way to his shoulder and Zict would gently stroke the fuzz on their heads before they fluttered off. He was halfway across the meadow when the satyrs finally noticed him. To his surprise, they greeted him with warm smiles.

"Welcome, stranger!" a satyr woman called, her curly

hair bouncing as she bounded towards them. "Come, join in our dance."

She reached her hands out and took his walking stick. The satyr who she had been dancing with helped Ciaran remove his pack. When Ciaran looked the satyr in the face, he saw a wide beaming smile. The satyr's hair was a nest of curls and poking out were two horns. They were also curved and their ends were rounded rather than sharp. Free from his pack, Ciaran stepped forward and took the hands of the woman who began to dance with him. He was unfamiliar and unpracticed with dance, but the satyr guided him, making it seem easy. Ciaran soon became so engrossed in the activity, he lost track of time. As abruptly as it had begun, the dancing ended, and he was left standing on the edge of the pond.

As Zict had said, the music stopped as soon as the sun had set. Bathed in the cool blue light of the moon, the meadow still had a charm and was beautiful in a completely different way. Each of the flowers still seemed vibrant, but their shades and hues were dark and cool. Ciaran stood, stunned for a moment as he witnessed all the color.

"It has been a while since a human has wandered into our wood. It was a welcome surprise to have you join us today," the satyr woman said.

"Thank you for allowing me to join."

"Of course. My name is Reri, what is yours?"

"Ciaran."

"And your small companion. What is your name?"

"Zict," the goblin answered.

"Well, it is wonderful to make your acquaintance, even for as brief a time as this. Tell me, what brings the two of you into our glade today?"

"I am on an errand to retrieve pigments to make paint for my master."

"So, you are an artist? How wonderful."

Reri's voice carried and it seemed as though it drew the attention of all who were standing around the pond. Ciaran didn't feel uncomfortable beneath their gaze like he'd expected. Instead, he found their smiling faces to be welcoming. All the satyrs seemed as genuinely enthralled to see him as he felt towards them.

"Will you paint for us?" Reri asked.

"I do not have brush nor paint to do so," Ciaran replied. "Nor do I have the skill or talent to make anything worthy of showing such wonderfully talented company as all of you."

"You do not have to impress us," Reri said with a laugh. "Here, take this."

The satyr reached into her skirts and from a hidden pocket removed a long brown reed. The tip was rounded and tipped with a golden band that held dark brown brush hairs in place. Reri set the strange paintbrush in his hand.

"What do I use for paint?"

"Well, the water of course," Reri answered.

She produced a small cup from her skirts, then bent over and dipped it into the pond. When it emerged, the water within seemed to swirl with every color Ciaran could imagine. Reri handed Ciaran the cup. Retrieving his sketchbook, he sat down, opened to the first blank page, and then got the new paintbrush ready by dipping it in the water. He felt an odd sense of pressure to perform, like whatever he produced had to be magnificent and representative of only the best to which he was capable. This caused him to freeze, the wet brush hovering above the page.

"Relax, Ciaran," Zict said. "Just trust yourself and be spontaneous."

Letting out the breath he hadn't realized he'd been holding, Ciaran let the paintbrush fall to the page. The colored water seemed to live as he spread it across the paper. The brush changed size and shape, seeming to follow his will and desire. Within moments, the splotches of dark greens and browns were transformed into trees and bushes. Blue erupted near the top of the page, spreading out like a clouded sky. The watercolor blended and flowed with ease and Ciaran allowed himself the freedom to paint as it came naturally. The experience was odd at first and part of his mind worried that at any moment he would make a wrong stroke and ruin the wonderful work that had come before.

When Ciaran lifted the brush from the page for the last time, he looked at the painting and watched as the watercolor dried. The final result was breathtaking. It was detailed in places, but for the most part, the colors gave off the vague impressions of a forest. Unwittingly, Ciaran realized he had painted the meadow that surrounded him.

"How wonderful!" Rerir cried out, clapping. "Please, paint another!"

The other satyrs gathered and sat down beside him in a

circle. Turning to the next page, Ciaran dipped the brush in the bowl of multi-colored water, and set out to paint. He lost himself to the work once again, and time lost all sense and meaning. Ciaran painted one picture after another until his eyes grew heavy and he could hardly hold the brush any longer. He smiled, examined the purple bell shaped flowers he had just painted, then set down his brush. Closing the sketchbook, Ciaran tucked it under his arm, then laid down to rest. While he wanted to keep painting, he was too tired to continue. He laid down, resting his head on the grass, and closed his eyes. Sleep took him in her gentle arms and in his dreams, Ciaran continued to paint.

It was the warmth of the sunlight which roused Ciaran from his slumber. Opening his eyes, he looked up at a brilliant blue sky. He was warm beneath his blanket and sitting up, Ciaran stretched both his arms. He looked at the pond and noticed that the satyrs were gone. Even though there had been so much dancing the evening before, the grass around the pond looked completely undisturbed; like it had never happened.

Zict was sitting on a rock which was partially submerged in the pond. He seemed lost in thought and he held a long blade of grass in his hand which he kept flicking.

"Good morning. How are you feeling?" Zict asked.

"Well rested."

"Great. It looks like they decided to leave you a gift."

Zict pointed to Ciaran's pack which was set a few feet away. Sitting on top was the reed brush Ciaran had used the evening before and the strange cup which had been filled with the watercolor paint.

Getting to his feet, Ciaran went over and picked up his gifts. The brush was smaller than he remembered, but as beautiful, with the golden band holding the brush hairs in place. The cup was different and Ciaran realized it looked more like a shell. Now that it wasn't filled with water, he could see that the bottom was carved out, creating more than a dozen small holes. Inside each of the holes was a hard cake of color. It was, to his amazement, a complete palette of paints.

"I never knew paints like this existed," Ciaran said, looking at Zict who was perched atop his sketchbook.

"Those are special paints. Used by the nymphs, satyrs, and other wild creatures. You must have impressed them."

"I suppose now, I will have something to practice my painting with on our journey."

"You better. I think they would be disappointed if you didn't."

Ciaran carefully packed the new paintbrush and paint away in the artist's bag, then looked back over at Zict who was now standing on his rock.

"Are you ready to continue then?"

"After I make myself a little breakfast," Ciaran said, opening the top of his travel pack. "I'm absolutely famished."

5
THE MOONWEAVERS

Dark, dreadful, and loathsome were the first three words that entered Ciaran's mind when he saw where the path ahead was leading them. Gone were the large trees that allowed warm daylight to pass through their leaves and branches. Now, he was faced with a dark wood, filled with trees that had sharp branches and such a thick canopy that no light seemed to be able to find its way through. A cold wind blew out from the wood and Ciaran shivered. He looked at Zict, who was perched on his shoulder, and tried to see if the goblin also felt fear. But those dark beady eyes betrayed no such emotion. Zict looked perfectly calm, almost happy, as he squatted on Ciaran's shoulder.

"I don't want to go in there," Ciaran admitted.

"Why not?" the goblin asked.

"Well, for one, how am I going to see? It's as dark as night in there and I can only see a few dozen feet ahead."

"Don't worry about that," Zict said, patting him with his tiny hand. "I can guide you so you won't get lost. Goblins can see just as well in the dark as you humans can during the day. Perhaps even a little bit better."

"But what about the things that live in there? I've heard stories of dangerous, man-eating, creatures that lurk in dark places, waiting to devour wayward travelers."

"It is a good thing you are not a man then."

"I am too," Ciaran protested, then after a pause, added, "almost."

"Well, you will almost be in danger. Trust me, I know these woods. They were my home when I was as young and inexperienced with life as you. No harm will come to you so long as I am by your side." Zict chuckled. "Or on your shoulder."

"Fine, I trust you. Just make sure I don't trip and fall."

"Don't you worry. Now get going. It is quite a walk through to the other side. We are almost at the first place to get one of the materials for your paints."

The thought of finding the first pigment gave Ciaran a bit of encouragement. That would put him one step closer to finishing this journey. Without a moment more of hesitation, he strode forward and passed from the warm sunny wood into the darkness.

Zict guided him as he had promised, making sure he didn't trip. To his surprise, his eyes did adjust after a few miles of walking. At first, he thought some light was spilling through and he began looking around. There was no such beam of light or any sign of the sun through the darkness overhead. Instead, he found that there were smaller sources of light coming from the ground. It was difficult to see them at first, the light just barely more than a dull white glow. But as Ciaran continued to wander, the path passed by an enormous black tree, and growing by its roots were glowing white mushrooms. The tops were spotted gray and due to their size, the mushrooms hung to the side, almost like they were about to topple over.

"What are those?" Ciaran asked.

"Glimmer Mushrooms. Don't touch them. They are sticky and your fingers will start to glow. Really difficult to clean off."

Ciaran gave the mushrooms a wide berth as he passed. He was grateful for the light they provided while it lasted. Soon, things grew dark again, leaving him once more to rely solely on the guidance of Zict. Fortunately, the path didn't have large rocks or holes, so Ciaran didn't stumble. Without the sun, it was difficult to tell time and he was growing tired of walking. Still, he did not want to stop and rest in the dark, he kept walking and remained silent.

The chill of the dark forest vanished in a single step which gave Ciaran pause. The air that surrounded him now felt as warm as a summer's day.

"What just happened?"

"Oh, we're getting close now. We got a few miles to the caves where we will be getting the materials for your white paint."

"I thought we were going to get red."

"We are. But this was on the way. Red is the furthest

away, so we will get a few colors on our way, and the rest when we travel back. Just like a big circle."

"So, what exactly are we going to be getting from the caves?"

"Just a bit of webbing from the Moonweavers."

"Moonweavers? Webbing? No!" Ciaran stopped walking and folded his arms. "I'm terrified of spiders. I am not going into a cave filled with them."

"Why? Spiders are nice. Many of them have been my friends over the years."

"Perhaps they are nice to a goblin. They are not so nice to humans."

"Have you ever thought they aren't nice to you because you were mean to them first?"

"But they are poisonous and their bites can kill."

"Only some spiders. Not the Moonweavers. They are nice. You'll see."

Ciaran could feel Zict's small hand pat his shoulder.

"You've trusted me this far, haven't you?" Zict asked.

"I have."

"And have I let you walk into a tree, or a hole, or into some form of danger?"

"No."

"So, why won't you trust me now?"

"I suppose I am just wary of the things I don't understand. I'm sorry, but I can't really help it."

"I understand Ciaran. I was a young goblin once too. Compared to the goblin king, I'm still young. But sometimes I think that because of your size, you are more experienced than you are. Just keep going. I promised I wouldn't lead you into danger."

Ciaran didn't protest further, and continued to walk as guided. After a mile, or what felt like a mile of walking, light appeared through the trees ahead. It was more brilliant than the Glimmer Mushrooms and reminded Ciaran of moonlight. Strands of white light hung about, forming patterns on the trees and in the branches above. Realizing that the light was coming from the spiders webbing, Ciaran felt a prickle travel down his back. Almost like a spider was crawling under his shirt. Though he knew it was just in his imagination, he couldn't help but shudder.

"We're close. Once we get to the top of the hill, we will be able to see the caves."

Zict was true to his word, and when Ciaran reached the top of the hill, he could see the caves. Light emerged from the holes in the cliff, illuminating the otherwise dark trees which surrounded them. Ciaran still couldn't see the sky, but he was able to see the bottoms of the branches that grew together. They interlocked, weaving in and out like the patterns of a complex basket. Looking back at the caves, he noticed that most of the holes were small and would not be large enough for him to enter. His worry that these would be large spiders was abated, and Ciaran relaxed a bit. Then, he saw the large entrance on the right side of the cliff. It was tall and long. More than sufficient for him to enter. Before Zict pointed the way, Ciaran started walking towards it. Though he had no desire to enter the spider's cave, he didn't want to dilly dally about either. Better to get the hard thing done so they could leave, then worry, delay the inevitable, and experience the suffering anyway.

Zict said nothing when they entered the cave. The walls were covered in spiders webbing so fine and intertwined, it might as well have been silk sheets hanging from the walls. Ciaran couldn't resist their allure and found himself leaning closer to see the individual strands of webbing. His hand reached out to touch the web and Ciaran felt sharp claws dig into his shoulders.

"I wouldn't do that yet," Zict whispered. "They are very particular about these sorts of things."

Pulling away, Ciaran stayed in the middle of the cave as he continued to walk. The main tunnel of the cave opened up after a short while and the massive cavern was like the inside of a dome. Every surface shone from the glowing webbing, but the patterns were more brilliant and there was space left between them that showed the bare black rock beneath. He could see tunnels and other holes filled with glowing spider webs, but no spiders.

Ciaran was both fascinated and creeped out by the place. The longer he looked, the more his skin began to itch. Turning his attention away from the walls of the cave, he looked down at the ground. The floor was clear in the middle, but around the edges, there were small bumps, like the back of a toad. These bumps were like small cocoons of silk, but they didn't have the same glow. Instead, they took on a dull gray sheen, like they didn't have any color at all.

Ciaran froze as the spiders began to emerge from small cocoons of webbing. They were the size of berries and moved on their long sharp legs with alarming speed. Crawling across the ground, they surrounded him, leaving Ciaran with no room to take a step in any direction. Not a single one of the spiders crawled onto him, but they drew so close and were packed together so tight, they completely covered the floor of the cave. He did his best not to scream or stomp his feet.

"Hello friends!" Zict called out. He sprang from Ciaran's shoulder and landed among the spiders who parted, leaving him a circle of ground to land on. "It's so good to see you all. Where is Beety?"

The spiders began to move, making strange chirping sounds which reminded Ciaran of crickets. The sound was not as sharp as that of a cricket, and it made the hair on his arms stand on end. When all of the Moonweavers stopped chirping, the silence that ensued was dramatic. A group of spiders around Zict pulled away and a single black Moonweaver stepped forward. Ciaran couldn't see anything unique or distinct about the spider. It had the same long black legs, the four large eyes, and the round body. But Zict seemed to be able to tell the difference. The goblin jumped up, then rushed forward and hugged the spider.

"It's good to see you my friend! Oh, it has been too long."

Beety, the spider, chirped a response.

"I know, I said I would visit sooner." Zict pulled out of the hug, and patted his friend on the top of the head. "This is my new friend, Ciaran."

Raising one of his front legs, Beety gave Ciaran a little

wave. The gesture was so simple, so human, that Ciaran smiled and waved back. Beety chirped again.

"Right, sorry that we disturbed your slumber. I didn't realize what time it was. I hope you will forgive our intrusion then."

More Moonweavers made sounds which reminded Ciaran of a murmuring crowd. Then, a large number of them retreated, making their way back to the cocoons they'd emerged from. Still, a significant amount of the spiders stayed, but they gave them room which put Ciaran a bit more at ease. So that he didn't feel like he was towering above the remaining Moonweavers, he took a seat on the ground and removed his pack. Then, reaching into the artist's bag, Ciaran removed his sketchbook and the silverpoint pencil. Almost without thought, he began to sketch the cave that surrounded him.

It was beautiful now that he was no longer afraid of it. No tapestry, no roll of spun silk, or embroidered piece of thread had ever seemed as exquisite and intricate as what he saw all around him. Perhaps Ciaran was imagining things, seeing more than what was there; but as he sketched, he seemed to see more detail and not less. While he drew, doing his best to capture a small portion of the beauty that surrounded him, Zict continued to talk with his friend. Ciaran only listened to parts of their conversation. Unable to understand what the spider was saying, it became a little difficult to follow a single side of the conversation. When other spiders joined in, Ciaran found it impossible. So, he tuned them out and kept drawing.

The first page was filled with a general sketch of the cavern, small lines to indicate the general patterns, but it lacked the detail he wanted to truly capture. So, turning to the next page, Ciaran decided he would focus in on a single section of webbing. As he was half-way done with the drawing, he was startled by several long black legs that appeared over the edge of his paper. His heart leaped in his chest, then Ciaran forced himself to remain as still as possible. The Moonweaver crawled onto the page, the four large black eyes glistening in the web light. It examined his drawing, and to Ciaran's surprise, began to make small scratches on the page with both its front legs. Then, orienting itself so it was facing Ciaran directly, the spider gave him a little chirp.

"Greetings," Ciaran said, uncertain how else to reply.

The spider chirped back.

Ciaran smiled.

Tilting its head to the side, the spider started to tap the paper.

"Do you want to draw?" Ciaran asked. "Sorry, but you will have to forgive me. I don't speak your language."

As soon as the words were out of his mouth, Zict sprang up and landed on Ciaran's knee. The goblin strode to where the sketchbook was resting in his lap, then placed his hand on the edge of the page. The spider looked at Zict who gave it a small wave and a big thin lipped smile. Chirping, the spider gestured first to Zict, then to Ciaran, and finally tapped the page.

"Silk says that she likes your drawing," Zict said, "but, she says that you aren't doing it right."

"I'm sorry."

Silk chirped and then tapped the page again.

"What did she say?" Ciaran asked.

"Silk wants to know if she can show you."

"Of course. Here, let me turn the page so you can start on something new."

Silk, the Moonweaver, moved from the page to his knee, then Ciaran turned to the next blank page. He didn't offer the silverpoint pencil to Silk, figuring that she wouldn't be able to hold it. Instead, he set it down at his side and prepared himself to watch the spider work. She crawled back onto the page, chose one of the edges, and using her web, began to string it down the page. She formed a criss crossing of lines and then starting in the center, began to weave round and around. The movements were like most spiders, the many legs working together as she jumped from strand to strand. But there was so much more to her technique than what he would have otherwise supposed. It wasn't just a simple web. The patterns moved in a spiral of zigzagging strands that managed to be simple yet complex. Silk's movements at first were slow, but as the pattern progressed, she began to move faster. By the end, she was spinning the web so quickly that Ciaran could barely trace the movements. When she was finished, Silk moved to the edge of the paper and Ciaran was left to look at the finished web. Silk chirped, and Ciaran glanced at Zict so he could translate.

"She said, now you give it a try."

"I will," Ciaran said, picking up his pencil.

He did as Silk had, first forming the crossing lines, then, beginning in the middle, began to make the zigzagging patterns from line to line. He worked slow, not feeling like he needed to match the spider in speed. Glancing from the page with her perfectly spun web and his own drawing, Ciaran began to notice more of the pattern. As he continued, he began to grow frustrated. Though the lines were simple, they lacked the beauty and elegance of the webbing. He desired the color, the sheen, the fluidity of the design which he couldn't match with his own pencil. Only a quarter of the way done with the drawing, Ciaran set down his pencil and sighed.

Silk chirped.

"Why did you stop?" Zict asked.

"I can't get it right."

Silk chirped again. This time, the sounds continued for a bit longer than normal.

"She said that it's not about getting it right. You aren't supposed to copy, you are supposed to feel. See the next movement, place only the next strand where you feel it would be the best. You don't make a web by trying to place every piece perfectly. Once you have the vision, you simply need to focus on just the next piece."

"But all of the pieces are wrong."

Silk crawled over the page and tapped the edge of his drawing where he had left off. Picking up his pencil, Ciaran got ready to keep drawing. Silk tapped the page again.

Placing the silver tip beside her leg, Ciaran watched as the spider dragged her leg in a swooping line to the next spot. He did his best to trace the same pattern. This repeated over and over and the more he followed the spider's guidance, the easier it became. When the drawing was halfway completed, Silk moved to the edge of the page and Ciaran drew without her guidance. Every once and a while, she would crawl back, use her leg to indicate a small correction, and then move back so he could continue.

Lifting his pencil from the finished drawing, Ciaran took a moment to look at what he had produced. Though very different from the web that Silk had created on her own, it still was beautiful.

"Thank you for teaching me," Ciaran said.

Silk bobbed her head back and forth and made a sound that was more like a bark.

"She said, you are welcome," Zict said, leaping onto the page. "Great work Ciaran. You will be a Moonweaver yourself in no time."

Ciaran still had an urge to draw again, but as he looked around the cave, he realized that he could never truly capture the intricate beauty of the webs that surrounded him. Nor did he need to. Each was unique to the spider who had spun it. He didn't need to copy what the others had done, but instead, use their patterns to inspire his own. A small smile spread across his face and he placed his pencil back in the art bag. One of the bottles inside tinkled and Ciaran was reminded why they had come.

"Silk, may I ask you a favor?"

Silk barked again and nodded her small head.

"I am trying to collect color to make paint. It's for my master. Is there a way that I could get some of your web so that I might turn it into paint?"

Ciaran removed a jar from his bag and held it out. It wasn't large, perhaps the size of a tea cup, and the top was secured with a piece of twine. Nodding, the spider moved toward the jar as Ciaran removed the lid. She crawled inside, then left something at the bottom. It was more liquid than the web, and it had a brilliant white shimmer. He had never seen a white so clean and brilliant. Not even a fresh snowfall beneath a bright winter sun.

Another spider crawled up Ciaran's leg, and then made its way over to the jar. For the first time since he had started to draw, Ciaran looked around at the spiders who had not returned to their cocoons. He hadn't realized how many of them were watching, their large glassy eyes all looking at him. One by one, they crawled up, and left just a small drop of the white liquid in the jar. Once it was full, Ciaran placed the lid over the jar. As he was tightening the twine, Silk crawled up the jar and began to spin a web. This helped seal the lid and testing it, Ciaran was satisfied that it wouldn't spill.

"Thank you all, I appreciate your gift. I will have to return and repay your kindness."

The spiders barked and chirped in unison, then they returned to their cocoons, leaving him alone with Zict. Silk was the last to leave, joining another spider who might have been Beety. Closing his sketchbook, Ciaran placed it into his bag, then looked at Zict who was still sitting on his knee.

"Time to go," Zict said. "We should find our way out of the forest before tomorrow comes."

Retrieving his pack, Ciaran checked that everything was secure, then left the spider's cave with a smile on his face.

6

THE BIRD WITH GOLDEN FEATHERS

The thick dark trees formed a wall blocking the path ahead. A little bit of light shone through and Ciaran knew he was close to escaping the darkness of the forest. He searched the wall of trees for only a moment before he saw a small opening, like an arched doorway, that he could exit through. Walking into the gap between the trees, he made his way back and forth, passing through a dozen large tree trunks before he stumbled out into an open field. Daylight had never seemed as bright, warm, and welcoming in Ciaran's life as it was when he finally emerged from the dark wood. At first, his eyes hurt and he could only open them a sliver. Taking in a deep breath, he enjoyed the warmth of the sun on his face.

When his eyes did adjust, he looked out over the rolling hills. They were covered with yellow grass and sparse shrubs. Several rivers were flowing down from the mountain ahead, merging into one great river that he could just see off in the distance. He didn't recognize the land, though the mountain peaks seemed familiar. After a moment, he realized that he was on the far side of the mountains that loomed north of Umrithos.

"How did we get here so fast?" Ciaran asked.

"We took a shortcut of course. I wasn't going to lead you the long way through the woods." Zict answered, his large ears twitching. "Are you also hungry?"

"I could take a break to eat."

Ciaran looked around at his surroundings and seeing no boulders or other places to sit, he turned back and looked at the forest. The large wall of trees looked foreboding. Inside, the trees had looked black, but under the sunlight, they were only a dark brown with leaves of such a deep green, they looked wet. Several of the trees near where he was standing had roots poking out of the ground and one was large enough that it would work as a seat. Going to it, Ciaran removed his pack, artist's bag, and cloak. Wadding the cloak up, he placed it on the root and then sat down. It wasn't any less comfortable than his wooden kitchen chairs. Zict leapt down from his shoulder and took a perch on Ciaran's knee.

"What do we have?" the goblin asked.

Reaching into his pack, Ciaran removed several rice cakes, dried figs, a small wheel of cheese dipped in wax, and an apple. Zict examined each piece of food with nods of approval. His thin wide mouth curled into a mischievous smile and he kept glancing back to the small wheel of cheese.

"Do you want to open that for me?" Ciaran asked.

"I think I could help with that."

Zict used his claws to cut through the wax and he removed the cheese as Ciaran took a bite from his apple. The skin was crisp and the fruit sweet. He chewed and watched as the goblin held the cheese.

"You can eat as much of it as you want, Zict."

"What if I want the whole thing?"

"Then eat it all."

Zict opened his mouth wide and Ciaran got a full view of his friend's sharp black teeth. They were the same color as the goblins claws. Each was as sharp as a canine and curved slightly inward. The goblin took a large bite of the cheese, completely filling his mouth. Ciaran chuckled, then popped one of the dried figs into his mouth. The two of them ate with the swiftness of two hungry boys who were eager to finish their food so they could return to play. It seemed like no time at all when the food Ciaran had taken from his bag was gone. Taking the leftover wax, Ciaran put it back into his pack, and then got to his feet. Zict moved a little slower, his belly quite a bit larger than it usually was.

"Did you enjoy that cheese?"

"It's my favorite."

"Do goblins make cheese?"

"No. I have tried, but it's a little difficult to milk a cow when you are my size. Fortunately, so long as we live close to you humans, we manage to *acquire* some from time to time."

"And by acquire, you mean take without asking."

"Sure. But we always leave something in return. So, it's like buying without asking."

"What do you leave?"

"Coins, buttons, an old tool. Anything we think the cheese maker would find valuable. We goblins are considerate in that way."

"That does sound kind and thoughtful."

"We goblins are wonderful creatures. It's nice to meet a human who also sees it."

Ciaran smiled, but held back his laugh. He didn't want his friend to realize he was teasing him. Instead, he put on his cloak, packed up his things, and started on the road again. Or rather, followed a natural path that seemed to cut through the rolling hills towards the nearest stream. He desperately needed a drink of water.

When they reached the river, Ciaran drank, the cold water hurting his hands. He glanced up at the mountains where he saw the snow packed near the peaks. While it might have been early spring in the valleys, it looked like winter up on the mountain. As he was examining the snow, he noticed a shadow move swiftly across one of the white peaks and cliff faces. Craning his neck, Ciaran looked up and saw something fly in front of the sun. The dragon, with red scales and black underbelly, was soaring so high up, it looked as small as a sparrow. Fear coursed through Ciaran and he began to look for cover, worried the dragon would spot him and swoop down to claim an easy meal. Zict didn't seem to hold the same preoccupations. The dragon soared on, flying towards the mountains, and then disappeared over the peaks.

"That is the dragon that burned down the temple I told you about," Ciaran said, standing.

"Ah, I know him. What a strange thing for Avot to do. I wonder why he bothered."

"Wait, you actually know him?"

"Of course. He is the dragon lord of the mountains. My father's grandfather saw his hatching. Told us the story all the time. I should have realized that you were talking about old Avot when you told me your story."

"So, the dragon is nice?"

"That isn't the word I would use. More like, solemn and thoughtful. He must have had a good reason for doing what he did. Avot doesn't just go around burning things down. The dragons that enjoy that sort of thing live too far away for them to bother with your town."

"Still, I can't think of a reason to justify the destruction of priceless artifacts created by the best artists who've ever lived."

Zict barked a laugh. "Best artists who've ever lived? You humans think very highly of yourselves."

"Fine, best human artists then. Why do you suppose he burned down the temple?"

"I haven't the slightest idea. Why don't we go and ask him?"

"Why would we do that?"

"His lair isn't too far out of our way. Once we get all of the paint pigments you need, we could take an extra day to visit him. Wouldn't you like to learn why he burned down your temple?"

"I don't know if..." Ciaran trailed off, intrigued and terrified by the idea of visiting the dragon. "Will he try to eat us?"

"What? No. Dragons don't like skinny teenage boys who are nothing but skin and bones. Your bones would get stuck in his teeth."

Based on the earlier teasing, Ciaran wasn't certain if Zict was joking. He glared down at the goblin and saw no hint of amusement or mischievousness on his face.

"Perhaps, once I have everything I need for my paints, I will decide if I want to meet the dragon."

"Why are you so afraid to meet him?"

"What if he is angry with me and decides to light me on fire."

"I don't think Avot would do that. I've never known him to take out petty vengeance upon curious wanderers."

"What does he take his vengeance out on then?"

"Other dragons. He is very protective of his lands. You can be certain that there are many enemies who stay clear of this place because he is protecting them."

"I never knew that."

"You humans are such strange folk. So preoccupied with yourselves that you don't notice the obvious things happening all around you."

Ciaran nodded, understanding the criticism. At least, he had been very preoccupied with himself. In his fourteen years of life, he hadn't paid much attention to things outside his own life. "You make an interesting point Zict. Why are you so much better at it?"

"I'm small and not anywhere near the top of the food chain. To live as long as I have, a goblin must be vigilant, observant, and most of all tenacious."

"And a cheese thief."

"Oh yes. Most importantly, you must find cheese on a regular basis. It is one of life's pleasures that simply makes everything better."

"Well, it's a good thing I still have some left."

Zict patted his stomach and the smile that spread across his face was so wide, it split his face from ear to ear. "I can't wait."

Sitting on the edge of the river, Ciaran bathed his aching feet in the cold water. He was tired from the day's walk and they were only halfway to their next destination. Examining the cliffs miles in the distance, he thought he could see the large birds flying around their nests. They had a glow about them and in the late evening light, the cliffs were bathed in orange light that made them shine.

Removing his sketchbook, Ciaran wanted to try drawing the scene. As he started to look for his silverpoint pencil, he remembered the reed brush and strange paints he had been given by the satyrs. Deciding he would test them out, he took those out instead. Opening his book to the paintings he had done earlier, he was surprised to find how well the colors contrasted with the dark red paper. They might have been darker than they should have been, but he liked the way it made the flowers look. Turning to the next blank page, Ciaran dipped the brush in the river, then swirled it on top of one of the dried cakes of paint. He decided to go for a blue and uncertain what would happen, he smeared the paint over the paper. The color remained vibrant, the dark reddish brown a perfect backdrop. Encouraged, he looked back at the cliffs and began to paint what he saw.

It didn't take him long to create an impression of the cliffs. Though the painting lacked fine detail, it was still a good representation of what he saw. He liked how quickly the paint would dry and how easy it was to simply dip the brush in the river to clean it off as he switched colors. When he finished, the sun was setting and he had grown cold in the shadow of the mountains. Pulling his feet from the water, he waited for them to dry before putting his socks and boots back on. Zict was already asleep, perched atop his pack, hands resting on his bulging belly.

Laying down on the ground, Ciaran used his cloak as a pillow, and just looked up at the sky. He enjoyed watching the clouds and the way the colors changed due to the setting sun. Pinks, oranges, and yellows were complemented by several shades of blue. Instead of trying to study it, figure out how the colors layered over one another, Ciaran relaxed his mind and just focused on enjoying it.

Feeling that he was drifting off to sleep, Ciaran slipped his socks on so his feet wouldn't get too cold during the night. Then, closing his eyes, he slipped into a peaceful slumber. It seemed that the exact moment after he'd fallen asleep, he felt a prickle on his ear. Opening his eyes, he saw Zict who was shaking his hands and babbling something. Sitting up, Ciaran shook his head and tried to understand what the goblin was trying to say. Then, he saw a brilliant flash of golden light.

His heart leapt in his chest as an enormous bird swooped down and dove towards the river a stones throw down stream. The bird was bright gold and it glowed like a lantern. Its large wings spread out just before it landed on the water, its curved talons dipping into the water. As it took to the air again, Ciaran could see that the bird had a large fish in its talons.

"What is that?"

"It's the Aurivis," Zict answered. "They are the golden birds. He was much closer than I expected. Hurry, if we go while he is hunting, we can get the feathers for your yellow paint."

"Wait, we're going to steal from it?"

"It's not stealing exactly. They are just very protective of their nests. But they shed feathers and they don't care much about them."

"Let me put on my boots."

Ciaran was ready in under a minute and they set off towards the cliffs moving as swiftly as he could. The noise from his pack suddenly seemed loud in the night and Ciaran kept looking over his shoulder at the bird as it flew about. Zict directed him towards the cliffs he had painted the night before. They still seemed so far away. However, after they had been walking for less than half an hour, Ciaran found himself at their base. He looked over his shoulder and he could see the river where they had been camping. The Aurivis was still flying overhead and he dove back to the river.

"How did we cross the distance so quickly?" he asked.

"Sometimes things are not as far as they seem. This valley is quite an illusion. You will see. Just keep going to the cliff."

Rushing forward, he reached the cliff and at the base he saw it was littered with yellow feathers. A soft breeze came from behind and Ciaran noticed that the feathers did not drift around as they should have. In fact, they didn't even move. Crouching down, he picked one up and it broke apart in his hand, like it was made from chalk. Removing a jar from his bag, he took off the cap, then began to place the feathers inside. They broke into a powder at his touch and soon he had more than he needed.

"Why are the feathers like this?" Ciaran asked.

"Aurivis are strange birds. They were not originally alive, but instead were molded from fine clay. They were presented to the Goddess Umris who loved them so much that she took a golden hair from her head and used it to bestow life to the creature."

"So when they shed their feathers, they turn back into clay."

"That, and they lose their golden color, but they retain the purest yellow you will ever find."

Packing the jar next to the one filled by the Moonweavers, Ciaran looked at the other empty jars. He hoped that the rest of the paints would be this easy to collect. Turning to leave, he heard a loud cry from above. Ciaran froze, the hair on the back of his neck standing on end. He looked up just as the massive bird dove at him. Raising his walking stick, he prepared to defend himself. The bird was so much larger than he expected and he started swinging too soon.

In response to the wild flailing of Ciaran's walking stick, the bird pulled back, taking to the air once again. Flying around them in circles, the Aurivis kept its eyes fixated on Ciaran.

"What do we do?" Ciaran asked Zict who was shaking on his shoulder.

"I don't know. I think we made it mad."

"That seems rather clear. Why is it so mad? You said it didn't care about its feathers."

"It doesn't. We must be too close to the nest. Hurry, perhaps if we run away and hide, it will leave us alone."

Without hesitation, Ciaran began to run away. He had never been a sprinter and with the pack, artist's bag, and walking stick, the effort was even more difficult. Every step took more effort than it should have, but he moved at a decent pace away from the cliffs. Ciaran didn't need to look up to know that the bird was still following them. It was evident by the golden light which illuminated the path ahead. If Ciaran hadn't been so afraid, he might have laughed. Reaching the first river, Ciaran noticed that the far bank was covered in a fog that obscured everything past the far bank.

"Cross the river. Go into the fog!" Zict cried.

Leaping into the water, Ciaran did a strange high knee gallop through the water. Fortunately, even the deepest part of the river wasn't more than a foot deep, and he crossed to the far side quickly. The wall of fog glowed as it reflected the golden light from Aurivis. Sparing a glance over his shoulder, Ciaran saw that the bird was flapping its wings and hovering above the river. Then, he stepped into the fog and the cold wetness completely enveloped him. His world became gray, and though he continued to run, Ciaran did so without any direction. Soon, he felt completely lost and the silence felt haunting. Looking down at his shoulder, he saw that Zict was still clinging to his shoulder, but wasn't moving. The goblin was frozen, his mouth pulled back in a snarl.

"Zict? Can you hear me?"

He didn't respond.

"Oh no," Ciaran said, fear causing tears to well in his eyes. "What do I do now?"

✤ 7 ✤
THE IRIDESCENT POOL

Walking a little ways into the mist, Ciaran paused, a pit forming in his stomach. Zict still clung to his shoulders and was not moving. Reaching up, Ciaran placed his index finger on the goblin's head. The skin was cool to the touch, like his finger was on top of a stone. Not wanting him to fall off his shoulder in this strange frozen state, Ciaran lifted him up and placed him in his pocket. He felt a little bad about it, but if Zict did fall, there was a chance he would never find him again in the fog.

Scarcely able to see a foot in front of his face, Ciaran prodded the ground before him with his walking stick. He could hear the taps and it didn't feel out of the ordinary. Taking a deep breath, Ciaran forced himself to move a single step forward. The ground was soft beneath his feet and when he took another step, he didn't stumble into anything. The mist hugged him. Cold and damp, Ciaran clenched his fists and tried to summon the courage to keep going. He only managed to take one more step before deciding that he would rather face the angry bird. Turning around, he made to walk out of the mist. He took ten steps, then twenty, and then fifty more. Nothing changed about the fog that surrounded him. Certain he had not lost track of direction, Ciaran froze, realizing that he was trapped.

"Of course I would get stuck in the mist," he muttered.

Ciaran felt a wave of exhaustion crash over him and he wanted to just lay down and go to sleep. Being chased by the bird had only temporarily filled him with energy. But as the feelings of exhilaration faded, he was left with exhaustion and fear. It was the fear that won out against his inclination to lay down and try to sleep. He would try to find his way out of the mist first. Then, when he was certain he was safe, he would allow himself to lay down and rest. Letting out a deep sigh, Ciaran resumed walking.

He didn't pay attention to the direction, deciding that since he was turned around anyway, it didn't really matter. Instead, he just focused on moving in a straight line. The grass beneath his feet turned to sand, and then to small stones. Ciaran liked the way the small stones felt beneath his feet and the soft clattering sound they made as they scraped against one another. Taking another step, he passed out of the fog and found himself standing next to a brilliant turquoise pool of water. He could see all of the edges of the pool along with the pristine white banks, but everything beyond was still shrouded in mists. The small stones he had been walking on continued into the water. Reaching down, he picked one up and found that the top half was warm to the touch but the bottom half was cool. Turning the flat disk like stone over several times in his fingers, he stepped forward and flung the stone towards the top of the water.

The stone skipped several times before it sank with a distinct plop. Ripples disturbed the glass like surface of the water and when they reached the edges, there was just a slight sound of water lapping up on several of the stones. Studying the glowing water, Ciaran sat down, and looked at his reflection. His hair was a mess, a bit tangled, with several leaves caught in snarls. Combining the snarls and leaves from his hair with his fingers, he took a moment to examine them in his hand. Partially dead, the yellow leaves had five sharp points on either side and a longer tip that curled slightly to the side. Reaching forward, Ciaran set the leaf gently upon the water. It floated on the surface, causing a bit of the water to bulge around the leaf's edge. Blowing on the leaf, he sent it floating out towards the middle of the pond. It didn't move fast, but it had enough momentum to reach the center of the small pond where it remained.

Removing Zict from his pocket, he set the frozen goblin down on the ground. He hoped that his friend would start moving, but he did not. Instead, he remained as still as a stone.

"Sorry this happened to you. This seems like such a strange place. I don't remember seeing a pond like this before."

Looking back at the pond, he scanned the top of the water for the leaf. It was gone. Curious, Ciaran leaned forward and saw something moving in the water up ahead. The glow of the pool was brighter around the movement and as it drew nearer, Ciaran realized that it was a fish. It took him a few moments to recognize the type of fish. It looked a great deal like a Koi, but instead of the usual red splotches on a white body, the markings were blue. The fish scales also gave off light which Ciaran realized was the source of the illumination. Swimming closer, the fish made it within arms reach of the shore before it swam in a circle, then started making its way to the other side of the pond.

Getting as close to the edge of the water as he could without touching it, Ciaran looked into the brightness of the iridescent pool. What had first appeared shallow was in fact a rather deep pond, the floor covered in tall strands of some underwater plant. It reminded him of a mix of kelp and coral, neither of which would belong in a freshwater pool, let alone a body of water of this size. This increased Ciaran's curiosity and intrigue, making him wonder if the pond was salty like the ocean.

After a short time, the fish swam back towards him, and another blue spotted Koi emerged from the shelter of the underwater plants. The second fish glowed like the first, but as it drew closer, Ciaran noticed that the scales were not white but black. Each fish seemed to complement the other, like a reflection, the spots of color on opposite sides. Swimming close, the two fish moved side by side, and then went around in a few circles before making their way back to the other side of the pond. This repeated ten times, with a new Koi joining the swim with every lap the first fish made to the far side.

Soon, the entire pool was glowing so bright because of the fish, Ciaran felt like he was looking at the sun. But the Koi's light didn't hurt his eyes and he could gaze upon it almost without blinking. His curiosity was increasing as he marveled at the oddity of the fish. For a moment, he was tempted to reach into his bag to pull out his paints and sketchbook to try and capture the moment. But he resisted the feeling, instead remaining still and watchful. Ciaran knew he could never quite capture this moment, the way the fish were swimming, the light of their scales, the glow of the pool. So instead of squandering the moment in frantic desperation trying to capture it, Ciaran decided he would just take in a sight he doubted many had ever seen. Smiling, he folded his arms, leaned a bit closer to the water, and enjoyed himself as the fish continued to make their laps around the pool.

Counting twenty five fish, Ciaran watched them all swim a single lap together before, one by one, they began to swim back into the plants below. This took just as long, with only a single fish departing with every lap, until the same fish that had first emerged, or at least Ciaran thought it was the same fish, remained. As it was making its solitary journey from the far end towards him, Ciaran redoubled his efforts to study the way the fish swam. Memorizing the glow of his scales, he was determined to paint at least one fish the next day. Perhaps he could, in some small way, preserve an inkling of the beauty.

When the fish reached him, it did not swim in a circle as it had before. Instead, it came up to the very edge and poked the top of its head out of the water. When the scales were exposed to the air, they no longer glowed. But the color of the blue and white next to one another was vibrant. Ciaran thought he had never seen such a true blue in his life. Even the brightest sapphire or purest sky would be jealous of the color he now saw before him. Reaching out, Ciaran touched the fish with a single finger. The scales were hot to the touch, but not enough to burn him. It was like placing his finger against the side of a hot clay cup filled with tea. Several bubbles escaped from the fish's mouth, and then it pulled back into the water. Ciaran left his hand hovering above the water for a time, then pulled it back. When he looked at his finger, he saw that there was a strange residue on his skin. It too was the pure perfect blue. Rubbing his thumb and index fingers together, he saw that the color smeared. Almost instinctively, he placed his hand in the water to clean off his fingers.

The water was hot but not scalding. More soothing than any bath had ever been. The exhaustion that Ciaran had felt earlier seemed to vanish, leaving him completely refreshed. He pulled his hand free of the water and noticed that some of the color had washed away. Placing his fingers back into the water, he rubbed them together and watched as the blue residue separated from his skin and began to drift towards the stones. There it joined the dark color which covered all of the stones in the water. Intrigued, Ciaran plunged his whole hand into the water and touched the bottom of the pool. A thick layer of something soft covered the stones. Curling his finger, he moved it like clay and he pinched a piece free. Removing his hand from the water, Ciaran saw that the clay-like substance he held in his hand was also that pure blue.

Laughing to himself, Ciaran reached into his artist's bag and removed an empty jar. He didn't worry about the strangeness of how he had arrived at the pool and instead was grateful he had managed to find it. Filling the entire jar, Ciaran washed his hands off in the hot water, then sealed the lid with a piece of twine. Placing the new blue pigment jar next to the other filled ones, Ciaran couldn't help but smile. He now had three of the six colors needed. The thought of getting the others so he could begin to paint with them excited him.

As he prepared himself to leave, he picked up Zict, who was still frozen, and decided to hold him carefully in his hand. Gripping his walking stick in the other hand, Ciaran took one final look at the glowing pool. There were no fish swimming around, but the water still shined. He smiled, then went back into the mist and fog.

The fog turned from gray to yellow as Ciaran wandered. He could feel the warmth increase as he went and hurrying along, Ciaran finally stepped out of the fog and onto a grassy hillside. The sun was just rising over the mountains and the beams of early morning were warm on his face. Zict started to move, grumbling and squeaking.

"Release me human! I...I..." Zict trailed off and he stopped squirming.

"Sorry, was I holding onto you a little too tightly?" Ciaran asked, putting Zict back onto his shoulder.

"No," the goblin replied. "I just seemed to have forgotten where I was for a moment. I am trying to remember why we were running."

"The Aurivis chased us into a fog. But then you froze and didn't move."

"Oh. How bothersome. I'm glad you made your way out again. The wandering fog is a strange thing. Not a friend to goblins, that is for sure."

Ciaran looked over his shoulder to see the fog and found that it was gone. The rolling hills were familiar, and he could see the dark forest off in the far distance. Scanning the rolling hills and winding streams, he was able to spot the cliffs where the golden birds were flying. They looked so small now that they were far away. He doubted that they would bother to come and chase them again, though for a moment, Ciaran remained worried.

"I found something in the fog," Ciaran said. "A pond where I found something to make blue paint with."

"Ah yes. The pond with the Koi."

"How did you know about that?"

"Ciaran, please. We were destined to end up there. I suppose the wandering fog decided to be of some use. I didn't really want to climb to the top of the mountains in search of it. I think we have saved ourselves more than two days worth of hiking."

"Where is the pool?"

Zict pointed towards the tallest of the four mountain peaks ahead. "There is a small bowl shaped valley on the other side of that mountain. It's near the top and impossible to see if you don't know what you are looking for."

"Well, since I already have the blue, what is next?"

"Breakfast?" Zict suggested.

"Alright, but after that?"

"Sleep."

Ciaran rolled his eyes, but he was tired. The feeling of refreshment from the pool was fading and, though his stomach rumbled at the thought of food, he was more eager to rest. Fighting back a yawn, he sat down, and took off his pack. He handed Zict some cheese, took an apple for himself, and drifted off to sleep after three bites. Ciaran dreamed that he was a Koi, swimming in a glowing pond, not a care in the world.

8
THE EMBER GROVE

After three days of walking, hiking, and sleeping on the ground, Ciaran was beginning to miss his bed. Though Zict had proved to be an excellent forager, finding good food in the wild with ease, Ciaran couldn't help but daydream of his mothers cooking. He was thinking about sitting at the table for supper, a warm soup and fresh bread before him, when he nearly walked into a tree. Shaking his head, Ciaran stumbled back and muttered an apology to Zict.

"Sorry, I got a little distracted with my thoughts."

"Well, pay attention. You never know when the trees will decide they want to burst into flames."

"Wait, what?" Ciaran asked as he stopped walking. "I thought you said we were going to the Ember Grove."

"We're here."

"But, it's just a normal grove of trees. I don't see anything special about this place."

"Did you expect the trees to be on fire all of the time, did you?"

"I don't really expect trees to be on fire, ever."

Zict looked at him as if he had said something nonsensical.

"Anyway, I kind of expected something a little more magical about this place."

"Again, with the insults? The trees can hear you."

"I'm sorry. I didn't mean it like that. I am not as experienced as you are when it comes to the more magical things in this world."

"Or when it comes to art," Zict reminded, his large mouth forming a wicked smile.

"Now you are just making fun of me."

"Not at all. Just trying to remind you who is the master and who is the apprentice."

"Of course. What was I thinking?"

"Yes, what were you thinking about?"

"My mother's cooking."

"Now I understand. That is a worthy thought to get distracted by. I can't wait for you to introduce me."

"What?" Ciaran asked, a little surprised. "I thought you didn't like to be around humans. I live in a city with thousands of them."

"I was only joking. Partially. I don't enjoy being around a lot of humans, but I wouldn't mind tasting some human cooking!"

"What are you going to do when we have finished our journey?" Ciaran asked. "I mean, I see no reason why you couldn't join me. I would be happy to share my room with you if you did want to come live with us. Though, we might have to keep you a secret from my mother. I'm not certain how she would feel about having a goblin around the house."

"I was thinking you could just take me back to my village," Zict said. "It's on the way back. Then, you will know where to come and visit me should you ever feel the need to go on another adventure. Or learn art from a proper master."

"I like the sound of that."

The sound of a thick tree branch snapping made Ciaran jump. He clutched his walking stick, holding it at the ready. Several birds took to the air, cawing as they flew towards the cloudy sky above. A stillness fell over the grove and a profound silence followed. Ciaran kept walking, staying as far away from every tree as he could. He felt like at any moment, one of them would lash out at him. They didn't, instead remaining still like trees should.

A soft breeze began to make its way through the wood, rustling the leaves, swaying branches, and moving the underbrush. The scent of woodsmoke began to rise up all around, faint at first, like clothing once it had been dried beside a fire. It reminded him of home and Ciaran almost felt at ease. The breeze turned into a gale, and all of the trees began to groan as they shook back and forth. Growing stronger, the smell of smoke was joined by plumes that rose up from the ground beneath Ciaran's feet. The calmness that had initially filled him vanished, replaced by fear and a strong desire to run.

"What do we do?" he asked Zict who was clutching his shoulder. The goblin's sharp claws were digging ever so slightly into his skin.

"Just remain calm. She's coming."

"Who is coming?"

"The Ashroot Dryad."

Ciaran stopped walking and tried to keep as still as possible. The smoke continued to rise up from the ground, and then the bark of the nearby trees began to glow. Between the natural crevices in the tree bark, he could see embers and flames began to travel up the tree from the base. The progress was like watching a small trickle of water run down the street between stones. Not fast, but not slow either. Ciaran watched with fear and amazement as the fire reached the tips of all the branches, transforming the leaves to flames.

Embers drifted down like dust, turning to ash just as they landed on the lush ferns that covered the forest floor. The ash covered the ferns first and then the ground. After a few minutes, everything was covered in red-orange ash, reminding Ciaran of fresh paprika. The wind had stopped completely and though Ciaran was surrounded by fire, there was no heat. Uncertain of what to do or where to go, he remained as still as possible, expecting that any minute, something or someone would jump out at him.

"What are you waiting for, Ciaran?" Zict asked, his claws digging a bit into his shoulder.

"I don't know. What am I supposed to be doing?"

"Well, we need to follow the flames. Don't you see them pointing the way?"

"No. I don't see them."

As soon as the words were spoken, Ciaran saw a change in his surroundings. The trees were still burning as they had been, but the way the red light flickered was different. Yellows and orange sparks appeared, moving from tree to tree. Unfocusing his eyes, he thought that he saw hand-like shapes pointing the way further into the forest.

"Nevermind. I see them now."

Walking forward, an ember caught Ciaran in the eye. It stung, making him wince as he rubbed frantically at his eye. This only made it worse and tears began to well up and leak out the side. He muttered a few words that his mother would have been disappointed to hear him speak, then forced his eyes open. His vision was fuzzy, but he managed. Continuing forward, he kept a hand on his brow to prevent any more embers from accidentally finding their way into his eyes again. Following the flickers of light through the trees, Ciaran soon found his clothes, bag, and skin stained red by the ash. Glancing over at Zict, he saw that the goblins' clothes were similarly affected, but not his skin. The flakes of ash just didn't cling to him, sliding off without issue.

"Why doesn't the ash stick to you?" Ciaran asked.

"Just the benefits of goblin skin. Dirt and things don't stick to us. That's why we don't need to take baths."

"Wait, you don't take baths."

"Nope. But that's not important right now, Ciaran. Pay attention. I think she's angry with us."

"Why do you think that?"

"Usually she greets me. Instead, it seems like she wants us to make the hike through her entire wood." Zict let out a sigh and rubbed his ears. "Hurry up will you? I don't want to make her wait any longer."

Redoubling his efforts, Ciaran walked faster, following the light through the trees. He walked up a gentle slope and the ash made his boots feel slippery. Using his walking stick, Ciaran managed not to slip or fall. The trees were beginning to grow larger and more spread apart. Then, he made his way around a cluster of trees to find himself standing before a stump that was four times as wide as he was tall. Like the trees that surrounded the stump, it too burned, the fire existing in the seams and cracks of the bark and wood. Each of the rings on top of the stump also burned, the colors changing. He saw every single shade of red, orange, and yellow among them. The way the tree glowed made Ciaran feel like he was looking at something that was a living breathing thing. Sitting in the middle of the stump was a wooden statue of a woman so innately carved, Ciaran couldn't believe that so much detail could be possible. Then, the statue opened its eyes and Ciaran realized his mistake. He was not looking at some statue but at the Ashroot Dryad. Not knowing what to do, he dropped to his knees and bowed.

"Why do you bring this creature here, Zict?" a soft voice said.

Ciaran was taken aback by how the voice was so mild yet conveyed so much anger. It made the Ashroot Dryad sound disappointed in a way only an understanding parent could be. The only person he'd ever known to speak in such a way was his mother. It made a chill rush down Ciaran's spine and he couldn't help but wonder what he had done wrong. Nothing came to mind, which made him feel worse.

"Forgive our offense," Zict answered. "It was not intended."

"I supposed as much little goblin. But that doesn't answer my question as to why you brought a human into this wood. You know that is forbidden. You know what they have done."

"I know. But I thought you would be willing to make an exception," Zict said. "Please, I meant no offense."

"Why did you come?"

"We came here to ask for a bit of ash to make paint," Ciaran said, his voice a little louder than a whisper.

The Ashroot Dryad didn't say anything in response. Ciaran kept his head bowed, staring at the ash covered ground. He could hear the Ashroot Dryad get to her feet and walk towards them. Her wooden feet made knocking sounds with every step as she walked across the stump, like a cane on wooden floorboards.

"You can stand, human."

Ciaran obeyed, slowly getting to his feet. The Dryad stepped down from the tree stump and walked over to him. Standing face to face, he was a head taller than her. Remaining still, he clenched his walking stick in his right hand. Ciaran could feel his palm sweating which made the wood feel slick to the touch. Placing a hard wooden finger on his shoulder, the Dryad prodded him causing him to lean to the side.

"What is your name?"

"Ciaran."

"Tell me Ciaran, why do you seek ash to make paint?"

"Zict said that the ash from this grove makes a shade of paint that is the truest red. I am searching for only the best colors. He did not say that it was forbidden for me to come here."

"This is something I do not understand about you humans. Tell me, what is the purpose of painting?"

Ciaran paused, several answers coming to mind. But they were human answers. He remained silent for a moment while he collected his thoughts. Just as he was about to answer, the Ashroot Dryad stepped back onto the stump and placed her hands on her hips.

"Certainly you humans must have a reason."

"There are many reasons. But the answer that I feel is right seems too simple."

"Simple answers are often the best. Stop delaying and speak it, Ciaran."

"The purpose of painting is to take the beautiful things only I can see and transform them into something others can also enjoy."

"This doesn't make sense to me."

"Honestly, I don't think I understand it much myself."

"How so?"

Ciaran looked around at the burning grove and smiled as he looked at the burning leaves casting embers that continued to fall all around them. "I could never paint the beauty I see in this place. Perhaps I could capture a piece, a moment, but for every detail I can present, there are a thousand more that would be lost."

Reaching out his hand, he caught an ember and watched as it turned to ash in his hand. He then held it out so the Ashroot Dryad could see.

"Take this flake of ash for example. It was alive for a moment, a spark of flame that lived but a short life that has now ended. Captured in a painting, its beauty would live on. I can't explain the need I feel inside to create. Or why I feel it is so important. It gives my life meaning and I never feel more alive then when I am making something; even if what I am making is as short lived and seemingly insignificant as a dying ember."

The Ashroot Dryad said nothing in response and instead walked away and sat down on the stump. She placed her elbows on her knees and then rested her chin atop her hands. Ciaran looked at the sad contemplative expression, then walked over and sat beside the Dryad. Zict hopped down from his shoulder and sat on the stump between them.

"Ciaran," the Ashroot Dryad said, "when you look around at this place, what do you see?"

Looking at the burning trees, Ciaran smiled. He didn't feel like he needed to be quick to answer. Instead, he took a moment to examine his surroundings once again. The fire that flickered up and down the trees, making the branches glow, and leaves seem alive, was beautiful. He also noticed that they were ever changing. No single moment seemed the same as the one before. The longer he looked, the more amazed he felt about the entire experience.

"I see so much color, the way the flames flicker and bite and snap. Every moment is unique. I can't say that anything I have ever witnessed has such changing beauty as I have experienced in this grove. What is even more astonishing is that the fire doesn't seem to be consuming the trees. Instead, they exist in harmony with one another."

"This is a special place. An old magic runs deep, preserving this forest as it was. The trees here do not grow, they do not change, they do not die. But the fire that lives within them is always new, ever changing, it's life short lived. We are approaching the end of the hour in which they burn. Soon, all will return to how it was before, completely unchanged."

"How wonderful," Ciaran said, a wide smile spreading across his face.

"Why do you think that?"

"So few things remain the same for long. I love the idea that this place is allowed to remain the same. What a precious gift."

"I see. Zict, you did well in bringing this human here. So few of their kind truly see. They think they understand, and in their hurry to be about their lives, they don't take the time to simply see the things around them."

"So, will you give us ash to make the paint?" Zict asked.

"Of course. I would do anything for you. And you, Ciaran, are also welcome to return to this place whenever you wish. It would be a pleasure to spend more time in your company."

"Thank you. It is an honor and I certainly will return as frequently as I am able."

The crackle of the fire stopped and the embers stopped falling from the leaves above. Wind began to rush through the trees, once again increasing the scent of woodsmoke. Then, the fire began to creep back down the trees. Ciaran watched them until they disappeared. As the Ashroot Dryad had said, the forest returned to how it had been before. Even the red ash began to blow away.

"Hurry, let's gather some red ash before it fades away."

9
THE CLAY SENTINEL

Ciaran followed the mountain trail, being careful to stay as far away from the cliffside edge as possible. Though it wasn't too far of a drop from where he was to the slope below, if he fell he would most likely land without hurting himself, though Ciaran wasn't eager to test it. He was only half way up the ridge of mountains and it had taken them two days of climbing. Looking to the two large peaks ahead, he wondered if he would have the strength to keep hiking. Soon he would reach the steep stone cliffs and that would make the journey all the more difficult.

Hiking until the early afternoon, when the sun was beginning its descent in the southwestern sky, Ciaran found that the trail ended on a small plateau filled with boulders. Relieved to not be walking along a cliff edge, he found a large boulder with a flat top and took a seat. The brown stone was warm to the touch. Removing his pack and artist's bag, Ciaran set them down on the ground, then laid down flat on the stone. It felt good to stretch his back and the sunlight was pleasant on his face. Zict, who had been napping in the pocket of his cloak, crawled out, and took a perch by Ciaran's head.

"I must have been tired to have slept through the morning," Zict said, yawning.

In the moment the goblin had his mouth open wide, Ciaran could see all of Zict's shining black teeth and gray tongue. When his friend stopped yawning, his large ears quivered and laid back which made him look a lot like a dog. Ciaran resisted the urge to reach out and pat the goblin on the head. This made him smile and he chuckled. Looking back at the sky, he began to watch as several clouds began to drift past.

"You laugh a lot," Zict said. "And always at the strangest of times."

"I suppose I find a great number of things amusing."

"Have you put any more thought into visiting the dragon? Just a few more days of walking and we will be close."

"He lives on the other side of that peak over there, right?" Ciaran said, making a slight gesture with his hand.

"That he does."

"And the other pigments we need are found between here and there?"

"Yes. We're getting close to the clay golems which will provide us with the brown we need and at the end, we will be able to take another shortcut through the glass caves.

From there, we can either go back to your home, or make the quick hike up to see Avot."

"You know what, I think I do want to see him."

"Good. I'm glad you changed your mind."

"Is he big up close?"

"Well, he's considerably larger than me."

"So am I."

"I know," Zict said. "But bigger. I think he will be as large to you as you are to me."

"Well then, I suppose that is a relief."

"Why?"

"I wouldn't be large enough to make a good snack."

"Of course not. I have told you this. There isn't enough meat on your bones."

"And there is definitely not enough meat on yours."

Zict took a step back and placed a hand on his vest. "What would make you say such a thing?"

The goblin sounded quite astonished.

"I was just thinking, if we get stuck up here with nothing to eat, I wouldn't want to have you as a snack either."

Pausing, Zict's ears began to twitch, and then the goblin started to laugh. "Human humor! I get it. So funny."

Ciaran watched as the goblin doubled over with laughter, then as suddenly as it had begun, it stopped. Zict looked at him with a serious expression and then held out a hand.

"Got some more cheese?

"Let's see what we've got left."

The two of them ate a sparing lunch and Ciaran began to feel a little anxious that he wouldn't have enough food for the journey back. Foraging had been a lot harder in the mountains and if they weren't careful, he'd have to make a long, hungry hike back down.

Still a little weary from the morning's hike, he lingered another hour, spending the time to sketch his surroundings. He'd already filled half of his sketchbook with drawings or paintings. Though it had not been his intention, the leather cover was beginning to look a little worn and the spine had a nice crease. But the leather was well made and the flap which covered the pages protected his sketches, which to Ciaran, was the most important part. In the end, it wasn't the cover that he wanted to protect as much as he wanted to protect what was inside.

Packing his sketchbook away, he checked on the jars of pigment and was satisfied to find that they were all sealed and none had cracked. The artist's bag was well made, with leather pockets for each jar which helped prevent them from sliding around or clinking against one another. Still, he felt worried that at any moment, he would accidentally break them. Shoving this fear away, he closed his bag and then got to his feet.

Zict jumped onto his shoulder and grabbing the walking stick and Ciaran set out across the small plateau. The boulders that covered the ground ranged from the size of a pumpkin to the size of a cow. Hardly a space was left between any of them and there was no easy path to the other side. Ciaran moved slowly, hopping from boulder to boulder, trying his best not to fall or twist an ankle. When he reached the far side, he saw that a trail had been carved in the side of the mountain. The cliff had a much larger drop than the one he had walked beside before and Ciaran felt his heart sink.

"I'm not sure I can do this," Ciaran said, shying away from the cliff.

"Just take it slow. Don't worry, we are on the edge of golem territory. They walk this path all of the time and they are much bigger than you."

"They are made of clay. A golem could fall without it being an issue."

"Sure. But they don't fall. At least, I haven't seen it happen."

Forcing himself to step forward, Ciaran started walking down the path and found that he did have plenty of space to walk. Still, he hugged the side of the cliff, his shoulder almost constantly pressed up against it. He tested the ground ahead with his walking stick, tapping portions of the ground that he thought might give way. To his relief and surprise, the ground was more solid than it looked. The dirt was better packed than a road and even the smaller stones were impossible to pry free. After a mile of walking, he relaxed and began to hike at a much better pace.

When he was half way along the trail, he began to feel a tremor beneath his feet. Placing his hand against the side of the mountain, he felt that the stones were also vibrating. It was like he had his hand against the side of an enormous purring cat.

"Zict, what is going on?"

"They are coming."

"The golems?"

"Yes. We've entered their land and the sentinels are coming to greet us."

"I don't know why I didn't ask this before, but are they friendly? I'm not trespassing by being here."

"No. We are not trespassing. And of course the golems are friendly."

Ciaran relaxed a little. "Good."

Remaining perfectly still, he waited as the tremors increased. Then, from above, a large ball of clay began to roll down the cliff. The brownish red clay clung to the stones and left a small residue as it went. When it was a dozen feet above the path, it dropped down and morphed into a man-like shape. The golem wasn't detailed, instead the lumps of its body making only the rough shapes of a head, torso, and limbs. It reminded him of a clay sculpture that had just been put together before an artist started a work of refinement. Part of Ciaran wanted to go and begin to sculpt more detail. It was a strange thought.

The golem held out a hand and motioned them forward. Ciaran obeyed, walking over to the golem. When they were within arms reach, he stopped, and waited. The golem still had its hand stretched out. Looking at the creature's face, Ciaran saw only the indications of a brow, but no eyes or mouth. Still, he felt like the creature could see him, or at the very least sense him. They stood staring at one another for a few minutes and the golem didn't move.

"What does he want?" Ciaran asked.

"Touch his hand."

"Are you sure?"

"He's been holding it out to you."

Reaching out, Ciaran placed the palm of his hand against the golems. The clay was cold and sticky to the touch. After a moment, the golem pulled away and his form began to change, additional detail forming from the clay until Ciaran was standing in front of a perfect clay model of himself. Even the details of his clothes were the same. However, the golem did not form his pack, bag, or walking stick from the clay.

"It has been a very long time since we had visitors," the golem said. Its voice was a great deal deeper than Ciaran's. "You have come at a very good time. The pool is all alive because of the spring season. Would you like to come with me to see them?"

Uncertain if he should accept the offer, Ciaran looked at Zict who nodded.

"We would be delighted to see them," Zict answered.

"I am glad. Please, if you both would follow me."

Turning about, the golem started walking down the path. He didn't seem at all bothered by the cliff's edge and with each step, the ground trembled slightly. Where each foot landed, there was a wet footprint. Ciaran wasn't certain if it was just a bit of moisture that made the path dark or if small portions of the golem were being left behind. But it suddenly became obvious why this path was so well packed down. Ciaran wondered how much the creature weighed.

Walking for a mile, they reached a crack in the mountain that revealed a split in the path. One path continued on and the other led up the mountain at a steep incline. The path that led upward was just wide enough for one person and after a few paces, there were stairs that had been formed from hardened clay. The contrast between the steps and the stone walls of the mountain were stark. Ciaran liked the way the brown clay complemented the gray and black hues of the mountain stone.

"This way," the golem said, starting up the stairs.

Ciaran followed and after about twenty steps, his legs began to burn. The golem walked fast, not the least bit tired from the effort of such a steep climb. Forcing himself onward, Ciaran kept pace with the golem despite the strain and burning of his legs. When they were halfway to the top, he cried out and was forced to pause.

"Sorry, I must take a moment to rest."

"My apologies. I had quite forgotten that you humans are more frail than we are."

The golem bent down and placed his hand against the steps and they began to move. Ciaran remained standing, but the steps began to rise up and he swiftly ascended the path towards the top of the mountain. Smiling in wonder and delight, Ciaran enjoyed the way the wind moved against his face as they picked up speed. The feeling was better than riding in a wagon or even in the saddle of a running horse. It was both fast and smooth, with no bumps to jostle him or make the ride uncomfortable. As they approached the top, Ciaran couldn't help but let out a cry of delight followed by laughter. When he looked at the golem, he saw that it was smiling as well.

"This is spectacular!"

Nodding, the golem smiled wider, showing perfect clay teeth. Ciaran felt like he was looking at a reflection of himself. When they reached the top and the movement of the steps slowed and then stopped all together. Part of him wanted to rush down to the bottom so he could experience it all over again. It was a thrill of something new and that brought a powerful unique delight.

"Thank you," Ciaran said to the golem. "I've never experienced something like that before."

"Come. The others would like to meet you."

The top of the mountain ridge where they walked was shaped like a trough. The sides were not tall, perhaps only twice Ciaran's own height, and when they reached the end, he found himself at the top of a bowl shaped crater. Mountain peaks and crags lined all of the sides and in the very center was filled with bubbling clay. Each time one of the bubbles started to expand, a bulbous form lifted out of the clay, and then it would burst with a satisfying pop. Steam rose from the popped bubble, and the smell reminded Ciaran of eggs that had been left out in a hot sun. Wrinkling his nose, he followed the golem into the crater, doing his best to ignore the smell. The closer he got, the more the smell grew until it was almost overpowering. Zict was humming on his shoulder, though Ciaran couldn't tell if it was out of pleasure or agitation. Not wanting to offend the golem, he decided he wouldn't ask.

Reaching the edge of the bubbling clay, Ciaran remained a few steps back from where the dried rust colored dirt suddenly shifted to a thick wet brown. The dried ground was covered in small cracks, the edges curled up slightly. Curiosity got the better of him and bending down, Ciaran placed his fingernail under the lip of one of these cracks. The entire section lifted up, revealing a semi-dry patch of clay beneath. Examining the dried bit in his fingers, he noticed that it had a rich color which would make an excellent pigment.

"My apologies," Ciaran started to say, but found that the golem was nowhere to be found.

He waited for a moment, and saw nothing change. Bubbles continued to form, burst, and then fall flat.

"What do we do now?"

"I suppose we will just have to wait. I'm certain the golem will be back."

"Where did he go?"

"He stepped into the clay. I suspect it will wake the others."

"I think," Ciaran said, lifting the piece of dried clay up so Zict could see, "that this will make an excellent brown pigment."

"You are getting good at this," Zict said. "It is precisely the reason we came. I once knew an artist who made all his paints from clays and soils. It will make a true dark brown."

"Do you think they will mind if I take some?"

"Not at all. Golems are not creatures who think like you or I do. They delight in creating things with the earth. You witnessed the stairs they made. Go ahead and gather some while we wait for our new friend to return."

Crouching back down, Ciaran took one of the two remaining bottles from his bag, and packed the dried clay into it. Dusting his fingers off on his cloak, Ciaran took the twine and tied the lid shut. Returning the jar to its proper pouch, he closed his bag and turned his attention back to the brown pool.

A few minutes passed and the golem didn't return. Not wanting to waste the moment, Ciaran took out his sketchbook and began to draw the edges of the crater that surrounded him. He moved his silverpoint pencil across the red page with quick strokes, concerned more with making indications of what he was seeing to save for a later painting. There was so much variety, just in the different shades of brown that covered the rocks, that he felt inspired to experiment and add variety with layers of markings from his pencil. Finishing half a dozen little sketches, Ciaran felt satisfied that he had captured enough ideas and reference to paint this place from memory. As he packed away his sketchbook, he heard a loud pop from the center of the clay pit.

A large bubble began to emerge and grow. As it expanded, it took on a more oval and then cylindrical shape. Bursting, the clay collapsed upon itself, taking a vaguely human shape, but without the correct proportions. Eight more of these cylindrical shapes rose out of the clay to join the first. Once they had all formed into human-like form, they remained still. Even as the clay around them continued to bubble, they didn't rise or fall. Ciaran found himself shifting his weight from foot to foot as he waited. He was still growing accustomed to the new experiences, but it no longer bothered him to wait. Instead, the experience excited him. Every passing moment only provided him with additional opportunities to see and observe the figures. Though he knew that it wouldn't be possible to remember every detail, the longer he had to look, the more he would remember.

Finally, a tenth form began to emerge, much larger than any of the others had been. Rising more than thirty feet into the air, the shape began to shift and expand until a giant of clay was standing before him. This, unlike the others, was correctly proportioned, just like the first golem had been. Ciaran wondered if this was the same one. As the surface of the giant golem continued to change, it became more detailed and more human. Even the texture of the skin was the same, with wrinkles on the knuckles and lines of the skin. The last thing to take shape was the face; and it was his own.

"This is my family," the golem said. "They are all young, little more than children. This is their first time seeing a human."

As the giant golem spoke, the others started to move, making their way closer. Ciaran couldn't help but take a small step backwards, the realization of their size making him weary.

"It's okay Ciaran," Zict whispered.

"Do not fear, they will not harm you. But I would ask that you would let them practice taking on your shape."

Ciaran nodded. "I didn't mean to seem afraid."

"Few ever do. But I understand. It is not always easy to stand up to things that seem much bigger than you."

Remaining still, Ciaran allowed the nine golems to approach him. Each remained at the edge of the pool of clay. They all seemed wary of emerging from the pool and their feet remained submerged. The golem closest to Ciaran held out a stump of an arm. Walking forward, he placed his hand on the stump, the warm clay sticky on his skin. At his touch, the golem took shape, becoming a little more human in appearance. It was only the top half that managed to adjust itself to the correct proportions. The golems legs turned even more stumpy and it sank down into the clay. Each of them took a turn, and each was only partially successful at mimicking him. When they were done, they returned to the middle, retaining their new shapes.

"I appreciate your patience, human. It has been a delight to have your company this day."

"May I ask something?"

"Of course."

"Would you be willing to stay where you are so I can paint you?"

The giant golem smiled and nodded his head. "We would be delighted."

10
THE GLITTERING CAVES

Riding on the shoulder of the giant golem, Ciaran couldn't help but smile. He glanced at Zict who was on his own shoulder and let out a little laugh. The goblin gave him an odd expression, and Ciaran realized his friend did not find the similarity funny. The golem moved along the mountain peaks with ease. Sparing a glance at the ground, Ciaran saw that the golems' clay feet would meld their form to fit against the rocks they stepped on. As a result, he was not jostled from side to side, making it feel like he was just sitting on a still platform.

From the mountaintop, Ciaran could see so far in all directions. He looked first to the valley they had come from, seeing the rolling hills and rivers. Then, he looked at the thick forest and was amazed at how the tops of the trees looked so interwoven together. He could even see the normal forest beyond and in the blueish gray haze of the distance, he could see the city of Umrithos. To his surprise,

Ciaran felt a longing inside as he looked at his home. He was excited to return and more than ready.

Since looking at his home was starting to make him feel a little sad, Ciaran glanced to the other side of the mountain and was astonished at what he saw. Rows after rows of mountains and valleys went as far as he could see. Some of the peaks were so large that they poked through the clouds, their tips obscured. Large rain clouds could be seen blowing in from all sides, lightning flashing. Ciaran waited to hear the thunder, but the enormous storm was still too far away.

When they reached the edge of the mountain they were currently walking across, the giant golem descended into the valley and then began to climb the face of the dragon mountain. Ciaran's anxiety began to increase with every step and he couldn't help but clench his fists.

"How far do you intend for me to go, little goblin?" the golem asked.

"We will be stopping at the base of the cliff just ahead."

"Which cliff?" the golem asked, pointing.

"Just to your right," Zict answered.

The golem moved, his finger pointing to a cliffside that was as smooth as glass and shimmered with a brilliant green.

"That is the one," Zict said.

Without another word, the golem continued on and within a half hour, they reached the edge of the cliff. Reaching up, the golem placed the palm of its right hand next to the shoulder where Ciaran had been sitting. Moving onto the golem's palm, he felt a little rush of exhilaration as he was lowered onto the ground.

"Thank you for taking us this far," Ciaran said.

"It was my pleasure. Take care my friends."

The golem turned about, then began to walk back. Its shape morphed from human to a blob of different limbs both human and not. Ciaran was awestruck by the speed at which it moved now that it had taken on a unique shape. He couldn't help but watch until the creature was out of sight. Thunder then sounded and Ciaran glanced to a darkening sky.

"Time to go, Ciaran."

"Where to?"

"Into the cave."

Ciaran looked behind him at the green cliffside. He saw no cave or opening.

"I don't see it."

"Just trust me. It's there. Walk forward."

Trusting his friend, he walked towards the cliff. When he was within arms reach he paused.

"Keep going, the entrance is just in front of us."

With a shrug, Ciaran stepped forward and just as his hand and walking stick were about to smack into the wall, he found that they passed through. It was a strange illusion and when Ciaran stepped all the way through it, he found he had entered a cave that was carved from dark green crystal. The shape was rectangular, and the walls were smooth. Ripples of color ran through the green walls. Examining them, he saw shades of blue, turquoise, and white hidden within the green.

"What is this place?"

"Just wait. You will see."

"Why are you keeping it a secret?"

"Sometimes it's okay not to know everything, Ciaran. Trust me, you will enjoy it more if I don't tell you."

"Fine."

Crossing the room, he found an entryway into a tunnel that sloped upward. Only the first part of the tunnel was made from the same green crystal. Then it transformed into a blue granite which was equally beautiful. He expected that it would get dark inside the cave as he continued up the tunnel, but a soft light drifted down from above. Looking at the ceiling, he couldn't see the source of the illumination. Ciaran could only see a bunch of specks that were caught in motes of light that appeared from nothing.

"Where is the light coming from?"

"Oh. Those are the Prismwing Moths. They are babies right now so you probably won't be able to see them really well, as they are very small. You will see the bigger ones soon."

When they reached the end of the tunnel, they passed through an archway and Ciaran found himself in a cone shaped chamber that went up into darkness. A spiraling staircase went round and round, expanding ever outward, eventually obscured by darkness.

"That is a lot of stairs."

"Yes. And these ones don't move on their own."

"We have to go to the very top, don't we?"

"Yes."

"Why?" Ciaran asked with a groan.

"Would you rather try to climb the mountain from the outside?"

"The golem could have taken us."

"Not in here."

"I meant on the outside."

"But what we came for isn't on the outside of the mountain."

Ciaran frowned, looking at the goblin. "So why did you say that then?"

"I was just saying, at least the stairs are easier than climbing cliffs. You should be more grateful, Ciaran. This journey could have been much harder."

"It's a little infuriating how you tend to win so many of our arguments."

"It's easy to win an argument when you are right."

Ciaran snorted and rolled his eyes. "I hope this will be worth it."

"Don't you worry. Once we reach the top, it will all make sense and you will finally have your last pigment."

"Fine, I trust you." Ciaran looked at the goblin then smiled. "It must be nice for you to ride around on my shoulder all day."

"It is quite excellent."

Walking to the stairs, Ciaran started the climb. At first, he took pleasure in the sound of his walking stick smacking down on the stone and the way it echoed all around. After the twentieth time, he grew tired of it and decided to tuck his walking stick under his arm as he walked. He tried to keep his attention on the steps directly in front of him. He noticed that on the inner side of the stair, there was another set of steps which were much smaller. At first, they seemed like a pattern, but the steps looked so intentional. Each step looked perfectly sized for Zict. What remained marvelous was how the whole thing was carved from the stone without any imperfection. Each step was carved exactly the same as the next, with no cracks or chips, and was perfectly measured.

Taking breaks as he went, it took him several hours before he saw the top. Counting the fifty remaining steps, Ciaran forced himself to continue even though his legs were burning. When he did reach the top, he sat down and looked at the stairs. No longer able to see the bottom, he wondered how many steps he had climbed.

"I'm exhausted, Zict."

"You should rest here for a while. We still have a bit of a walk left."

Zict hopped down from Ciaran's shoulder, and walked over to the edge of the stair. He peered over the ledge and whistled. The shrill sound traveled down and eventually faded.

"I have a question for you, Zict."

"Sure. What do you want to know?"

"Have you ever taken another human on this journey before?"

"Nope. Never."

"Has any goblin ever done anything like this?"

"Um, perhaps? I couldn't tell you for certain. My heart tells me that there is a high chance it has happened before." Zict looked at the steps. "This is an old place clearly intended to be visited by more humans than have come, but it rarely happens."

"Why do you think so few come?"

"A great question. I don't have an answer to that one."

"Not even a guess?"

"Of course I could guess at an answer. But if I were to present my guess as truth, you might go on believing something wrong. This journey is about learning and seeing, not about guessing."

"I think you are wrong. Without guessing, you might never open yourself up to trying new things. If I hadn't guessed that I could become a painter instead of a brick maker, I would never have begged my father for a set of paints. I would have never tried to make art. I think guessing can lead to amazing discoveries. So long as you are comfortable with the idea of being wrong."

Zict smiled and nodded his head. "See. I don't win every argument."

Snorting, Ciaran cracked a smile, then laid back on the gold stone. "Wake me in an hour, will you? I'd like to take a short nap."

"Of course."

❧

Ciaran dreamed of walking in spirals of color. Nothing seemed all that tangible and his head felt like it was spinning. The sound of eating that roused Ciaran from sleep and with a groan, he sat up and began to rub his eyes. Yawning, Ciaran blinked several times, then looked down at Zict who had half a wheel of cheese stuffed in his mouth.

"What do you think you're doing?"

The goblin shoved the rest of the cheese in his mouth and tried to close his lips around it. The cheese didn't quite fit and for a moment, Ciaran almost expected his friend to choke. But, as he always did, Zict managed to chew the cheese and get it down into his stomach. His stomach bulged and he patted it with both hands.

"Just enjoying a nice midday snack."

"You know that we only have one more, right?"

Zict's smile faded and his eyes went wide.

"I hope you enjoyed it."

"You can be certain that I did."

Zict got to his feet and hopped from foot to foot. Then he sprang up and landed on Ciaran's shoulder. He was so used to the goblin that it felt right to feel the slight pinch of the claws through his shirt. Getting packed up, Ciaran walked away from the stairs towards the entrance of yet another tunnel. The columns that lined the sides of the arched entrance had relief carvings of dragons on them. At the bottom was the tail and the dragon spun around the column until its head emerged to form one half of the archway. Ciaran felt his heart begin to beat faster.

"Is this the entrance to the dragon's lair?" he asked.

"No. The dragon's lair is on the next peak over."

"I thought this was the dragon mountain."

"Same range, just a different peak. We're close."

"If this isn't the dragon's mountain, then why are there dragon carvings?"

"Just keep walking. You will see."

Ciaran took a breath, adjusted his pack, then continued into the hall. The lights were brighter here than in the other parts of the cave and when he looked up at the ceiling, he saw small fluttering moths. Their wings glowed, giving off a soft light. Moving slowly, the moths fluttered from place to place, but always landed on the ceiling. Part of him wished he could save one in a jar and bring it home. Ciaran remembered how his mother had been angry with him when he'd done that with a beetle as a child. He smiled, and dismissed the idea. Instead, he just enjoyed their company as he continued down the hallway.

There were many passages on both sides which Ciaran ignored. His curiosity grew, wondering what the original purpose of this strange place was? When they reached the end of the hallway, it was blocked by a stone door. It wasn't made from blue granite but looked like a solid piece of jade. The entire surface of the door was polished and both stone carvings covered the entire surface. Ciaran recognized many of the wild animals which had an incredible amount of detail. The fur on the bear looked real and the feathers on the eagle almost seemed to flutter. Other creatures were depicted, some that Ciaran recognized and many that he did not. Among the largest was a dragon. This carving he examined much longer than any of the others, running his hand across the scales.

"Who made this?" Ciaran asked.

"Open the door and you will see."

Seeing no handle on the door, Ciaran placed his hand on it and pushed. There had not been a seam before, but as Ciaran pushed, the door split down the middle and opened inward. Even though it was made from thick green jade, it was easy to open, almost gliding as it moved across the floor.

On the other side of the door, Ciaran saw an open cavern that was so brilliantly lit, it was as if the sun were shining down from above. As his eyes adjusted to the light, Ciaran saw that it was just an enormous swarm of the moths clinging to the ceiling far above. Gaging by the distance, each of the moths appeared enormous, even the smallest was larger than a pumpkin. Little motes of sparkling dust drifted down from them as they lazily beat their wings.

The cavern floor in front of him was open for twenty paces before it ended abruptly at a series of archways. Between each arch was a platform that was the size of a table, carved from the same stone as everything else. Beyond the archways, Ciaran could see buildings and a city carved from the stone. In the middle of the arches and tables there were two buildings that stretched from floor to ceiling. Between them was an open gate through which Ciaran saw more of the miniature city. It went back into the cavern for at least a mile. All of the windows, doors, and patios of the buildings were small. Zict leapt down and let out a whistle. At the sound, hundreds of goblins began to emerge from their homes and the silence of the cavern was shattered. Hundreds of excited overlapping voices called out and goblins began to fill the tables.

"And here I thought you were the only art goblin."

Zict laughed, then scurried forward. "Come, we will go to the market tables where you can buy the final pigment you need."

Zict strode forward and moved surprisingly fast. Ciaran had forgotten how quickly the goblin could run since he'd grown accustomed to Zict riding on his shoulder. He walked after the goblin, careful not to take too large of steps and to keep his walking stick close by. They reached the first table which was already set out with different carved pieces of jade. Square pieces of finely woven cloth had also been set out and green powers were piled in the middle of each. Zict leapt from the ground to the top of the stone table with ease. He hailed the other goblins who returned his salute with ones of their own.

"A human, Zict!" a soft feminine voice exclaimed. "What a mighty surprise."

The goblin on the far right of the table stepped forward. She had silver rings running up and down both ears and a spike in her nose. She smiled wide as she approached. She was wearing a dark green dress that was laced with silver thread.

"We have come to purchase some pigment. This human is a painter and is looking for a vibrant shade of green."

Leaping to the side, the goblin pointed towards one of the piles of green powder. “This here will be what you are after. You could wander the whole world and never find anything of a more pure green.”

Ciaran smiled, then reached into his bag and removed the final jar. When he set it down on the table, the goblins' eyes went wide.

“Sorry, it’s quite large. But I am hoping to bring a lot home with me.”

“Not a problem at all.”

The goblin snapped her fingers and several others rushed forward. They took the jar back with them and began to use small silver spoon-like objects to fill the jar.

“How much do you want for it?” Ciaran asked, thinking of his three coins. It wasn’t much and he wondered if he could afford it.

“It’s been so long since we have traded with a human, I’m not certain.”

“How about, I trade you some cheese.”

The angry look Zict gave him was contrasted by the pure excitement from the other goblin. Fighting back a smile, Ciaran reached into his bag and fished out the final wheel of wax covered cheese. When he placed it on the table, the goblins all drew close, their black eyes going wide. Then they began to cheer.

II

THE DRAGON'S LAIR

Ciaran watched as a gust of wind lifted a pile of dead yellow leaves into the air, spinning it around in a spiral that was less than a foot off the ground, and moved it towards the sides of the path ahead. The warm wind was dry and his lips felt like they were going to crack. Despite the discomfort, he did not take a drink from his waterskin. Instead, he continued walking the path as he had before, determined to get this meeting over with.

Zict had been silent since leaving the caves and Ciaran wasn't sure why. His friend had been eager to leave and now that they had, Ciaran suspected Zict was actually sad about it. The moping expression on the goblins face was matched by the dropping of his ears. Uncertain what to say, Ciaran left his friend alone. When Zict wanted to talk, he would.

The peak up ahead was covered in snow which seemed

such a strange thing with how hot the valley was. Both ridges of the mountain ran close to each other and the valley where Ciaran walked was thin, with steep cliffs on both sides. The path was dusty and not very wide. Wind blew ceaselessly from the north and Ciaran spotted another spinning circle of leaves. Ciaran wondered what he would find at the dragon's lair.

Will it be filled with bones?

After a few more miles of walking, sweat began to drip down his brow. It was hotter now than the most sweltering summer day. Uncomfortable, Ciaran stopped and set down his pack. His back was sweaty and he felt rather uncomfortable. Removing his cloak, he felt a bit better, though the hot wind made the exposed skin on his arms prickle. Adjusting the belt of his tunic, he looked at his pack and the thick cloak that sat on top of it. The cloth was dirty, traces of mud or clay clinging to the hem. Even on such a short journey, it had begun to show signs of wear.

"Zict, how much further is the lair?"

"Not far. See the gap up ahead where the cliffs grow narrow?"

Ciaran looked and saw how the cliffs up ahead almost formed a triangle. The tips did not touch, but they were close to doing so. "Yes, I see the gap."

"Just on the other side of that is the lair. We are close, very close."

"Is it going to keep getting hotter than it is now?"

"Perhaps a little."

"Can I leave my pack here?"

"I would bring it with us. Unless you want to have to walk all the way back which I don't recommend. It will be faster to leave out the other tunnels than to backtrack."

With a reluctant sigh, Ciaran bundled his cloak, stuffed it under the leather strap which held the top flap of his pack closed, then slung it over a single shoulder. Though it was heavy and caused him to lean a bit to one side, not having the pack pressed against his back helped with the heat. He walked another quarter of a mile and then finally drank some water. It was warm, but that didn't matter. It helped soothe his dry throat and the moisture on his lips was a welcome relief from the discomfort.

"Do you want a little water?" Ciaran asked, holding the top of the water skin close to the goblin.

Zict took a little sip and then muttered a thanks.

Cramming the cork into the top of the waterskin, Ciaran decided to hang it from his belt so it would be easier to get to. He wanted to conserve as much of it as possible, but if the heat persisted, he was worried he would drink it all within an hour.

With renewed determination, Ciaran continued onward, focusing on each step while he did his best to ignore the heat. When he reached the gap where the two sides of the cliff almost met, Ciaran's shirt was soaked with sweat and he was completely zapped of strength. It took determination and his full focus to continue putting one foot in front of another. There was a short incline ahead and as he marched up to the top, his legs began to burn. When he reached the top of the incline, he stopped to catch his breath. What he saw made him gasp.

The lair before him was a large hole in the center of the mountain that, aside from the gap, was encircled by sharp peaks. The hole formed a near perfect circle and the black stone walls were smooth like glass. Ciaran guessed that the lair was a mile in diameter. When he looked at the ground, he felt his heart drop. The entire floor was covered in deep cracks with fire burning between each section of black stone. Ciaran didn't see treasure or bones or much of anything. And then, he spotted it. It wasn't in the very center, but instead built against the eastern side of the hole. The tower was hundreds of feet tall and the top was pointed. It was built from a dark material that almost matched the glassy black walls of the mountain. He saw no windows in the tower, but at the very bottom, he saw a large entrance with a pointed arched top and twin dragon statues on either side.

"Is that the lair?" Ciaran asked.

"Yes," Zict answered, his voice little more than a whisper.

"I did not suspect this to be so difficult."

"Neither did I."

"Was it like this last time you came here?"

"No. The fires have not been this alive in a very long time. Not since my grandfather came to watch the hatching."

"Does that mean another dragon is about to hatch?"

"It is possible. But I don't know for certain."

"I don't see a good way through the flames. How are we supposed to get to the lair."

"Give me a moment. I am thinking."

Ciaran was quiet while he let the goblin think. In the silence, he began to study the fiery landscape below. Ciaran looked at the cracked and broken stone and noticed that the fire did not emerge consistently from the cracked ground. Instead, it would spring up one moment and disappear the next. The fire moved and flowed. It wasn't unlike the fire he had seen in the Ember Grove.

He took out his sketchbook and then sat down to draw. The ground was warm but not uncomfortable to sit on. He started to draw the ground and quickly had a small map of the cracks. He then began to watch the fire, notice how it moved and sprang up from place to place. Though the flames were never the same, they followed a spiral pattern, moving in circles around the hole. Ciaran made small markings, noting which sections were best and would provide the most time for him to cross between the cracks. The path forward then seemed simple. He held his drawing up to Zict for confirmation.

"What do you think of this? If we follow this pattern, we should be able to make it through."

Zict reached out and tapped the paper as he watched the flames. "You did well. I agree. That should work."

"Let's get going then."

Ciaran tore the page from his sketchbook before returning it to his bag. He held the loose sheet of paper in his left hand, then got to his feet, and started down the slope towards the first crack. As the fire sprang up, it towered above him, bathing his face in stifling heat. When the fire disappeared, Ciaran ran forward and leapt across the crack. He skidded to a stop on the other side and used his walking stick to keep balance. His heart thumped in his chest and turning back, Ciaran watched as the fire roared to life again. With a deep breath, he looked down at his paper, then made his way to the next section. He stood in wait, and the moment the flames died down, he leapt across and landed again with safety.

He did this dozens of times, moving as quickly as he could while ensuring that he kept himself safe. Several times, he paused, uncertain, only to find that the fire sprang back up to life when he would have otherwise been in the air. Eventually, he began to feel like he understood the fire, could sense how it was going to move, and therefore, was able to keep himself from being burned. Ciaran's feet were beginning to grow hot and the soles of his shoes would stick on the black stone from time to time. Sweat no longer dripped from his body and a thin layer of soot covered his exposed skin, making him look greasy. The tips of his fingers were growing black and his fingernails looked dirty. The red paper was also growing difficult to read, the soot darkening the color and causing his drawing to fade. He felt as if the air was completely devoid of any moisture and this added to his sense of thirst. Taking breaks every few jumps, Ciaran drank from his waterskin as sparingly as he could. Still, he was running low and he'd only crossed half of the distance to the lair.

Zict had grown quiet and still. The goblin clung to his shoulder tightly, the small body pressed up against Ciaran's shirt. His eyes were closed and his ears were laid back against his neck.

"How are you doing?" Ciaran asked, his voice so dry it sounded old and withered.

"Fine," Zict muttered. "We should not have come here. I was a fool for suggesting it."

"No, you were not a fool. These things happen. We are going to make it."

Zict hummed and his eyes opened a bit. "We should get going then. I fear that should we continue to linger, we will perish in the flames."

Not needing any encouragement, Ciaran went to the next edge and waited for the fire to stop. The moment it vanished, he hurled himself across the gap and ran to the next edge. He didn't stop, he didn't hesitate, instead moving as swiftly as he could from platform to platform, eager to reach the lair. Several times the flames moved too fast to be avoided and Ciaran was singed for just a moment. The fourth time this happened, Ciaran lost his grip on his walking stick. He cried out as it tumbled away and then fell into a crack. Rushing over, Ciaran tried to retrieve it, but saw the flames as they began to emerge. Leaping back, he didn't make it away in time and his arm was caught by the fire.

Pulling away, he froze, half expecting pain. Looking at his hand, he was relieved to see that his skin remained unburned. However, his shirt was on fire. His clothes smoked as he patted the flames away. He looked at the back of his hands and arms and noticed that most of his hair was gone. Otherwise, he was relieved to find no harm had come to him. Realizing that the loss of his walking stick was preferable to the loss of anything else he carried, Ciaran continued on, redoubling his efforts to be safe over being fast. He didn't want to get burned or lose anything else.

It was a relief when he leapt across the final crack and found himself at the base of the dragon's lair. He marveled at the black tower and examined the stones. None of them were the same size or shape, but they were placed so perfectly together that they did not have any gaps between them. The two dragon statues that stood on either side of the arched entryway were enormous, and themselves were taller than his home. They were both carved from a single block of gray marble and the detail was as exquisite as the door that led into the goblin city he'd just visited. Ciaran wanted to stay and admire them, but he needed to get out of the heat.

When he took another step forward, his legs gave out and he lost all of the remaining strength within. It didn't even hurt when Ciaran landed face down on the slick black stone ground. He moved his fingers, trying to summon both the will and the strength to move. Ciaran struggled, attempting to pull himself to his feet. Ciaran only managed to slide his thumb back and forth, the glossy surface of the ground strangely soothing. Closing his eyes, he gave in to his exhaustion, and felt the heavy embrace of sleep envelop him.

As his mind drifted in the void of unconsciousness, Ciaran didn't fully fall into sleep. He could still hear the crackle of the fire. He laid still, too tired to think, let alone move. After a time, he could feel his body move and his arm dangle as he was hoisted into the air. For a moment he felt like he was flying.

12
THE LORD OF THE MOUNTAIN

Ciaran awoke in a soft bed. He kept his eyes closed and rolled over to the other side, his hand grasping for a quilt. Instead, he felt something soft. Pulling it closer, he snuggled with the unfamiliar blanket, wondering why his mother had put it there. Just as he was drifting back to sleep, Ciaran remembered that he had left home on a journey. Opening his eyes, he sat up, and found himself in an enormous bed. The bed was pressed up against the wall of a sizable room, lit by a small fire in the corner. The hearth and mantle were silver, and the fire that burned inside was such a fine mixture of red and blue that the overlapping flames looked purple. It cast a strange glow on the bed and upon the blankets. The blankets he had been wrapped in weren't black, but the color was so dark that in the strange purple firelight, he couldn't quite tell which color they really were.

Quite comfortable under the blankets, Ciaran remained where he was for a time. He had missed resting in a bed and he felt no urgency to seek out his host. Though, with every passing minute, he was growing curious about the dragon's hospitality. The longer he laid there, the more he wondered how such a large creature could have managed to get him through the wooden door. Though large by human standards, it would be far too small for the large red dragon he'd seen fly over Umrithos to enter. Ciaran realized that Zict wasn't in the room with him. He felt a little guilty that it had taken him so long to remember his friend.

It was worry for Zict that finally drove Ciaran out of his bed. He wanted to know that the goblin too was safe. Pulling the blankets off, Ciaran looked down and saw that he was dressed in a red tunic with black trousers. His socks had also been changed and they were soft but thick. Sliding his legs over the side of the bed, he stood and stretched. His back popped and the shoulder muscles by his neck were stiff. Yawning, Ciaran got to his feet and crossed the room.

The door had no handle and the dark brown wood had been polished so well, the surface was glossy and reflective. Purple light from the fire moved across the door, highlighting the braided band carvings around the edges. Uncertain how to open the door, Ciaran decided to give it a little push. To his relief, the door swung open about half way before stopping against a wall. The hallway outside curved left. Poking his head out, Ciaran saw that it continued to curve around the room. Silver sconces on the walls held metal torches which burned with the same purple fire that had been inside the room. Walking down the hall, Ciaran found a stairwell which went down twenty steps before reaching another flat landing. He descended them slowly, part of him not wanting his footsteps to be heard. When he reached the bottom of the stairs, he kept walking until he passed another wooden door.

Hesitating, Ciaran looked at the door and decided to knock. Standing with his back against the wall, he waited for a few minutes, listening for the sounds of movement. He heard nothing. After five minutes of waiting, he decided he would knock again, this time with a little more force. The three loud raps went unanswered, so Ciaran decided he would move on. There seemed little point in waiting around outside an empty room.

At the end of that hall was another staircase, just below the first. It too had twenty steps which Ciaran went down as carefully and quietly as he had done before. He strode down this hallway and passed another door that was the exact same as the previous one.

How boring, Ciaran thought, not bothering to knock.

Descending almost twenty landings, Ciaran was beginning to feel like he was trapped in an endless spiral. Just as he was beginning to grow frustrated, he reached the top of another staircase and at the bottom saw that it ended in an archway rather than another hall. The space beyond was mostly blocked from view, but the sound of a large crackling fire echoing denoted a much larger room beyond the archway. Deciding to forgo stealth, Ciaran hurried down the steps and out into the new room. He made it only two steps before pausing, his jaw dropping in surprise and amazement.

An enormous vaulted ceiling was supported by four rows of pillars. The middle of the room had a large rectangular floor that was made of solid gold. Between each of the pillars on the right and left walls were tear-shaped hearths, all of them filled with different colored fire. There were two doors in the middle of the long walls, both of which were closed. On the far side was a throne made from gold and glass. It glittered and reflected the firelight, casting rays of light onto the far wall. The flickering flames made the light dance and the image it projected was of a dragon flapping its wings. It was the most beautiful and creative masterpiece Ciaran had ever seen. Nothing he'd ever imagined before had come close to what he now saw. He was so awestruck at the wonderful image, that he stared at it for ten minutes without moving. Ciaran didn't even notice that he was not alone in the room until a hand gently took hold of his shoulder.

"It is good to see someone genuinely delighted by my work," a deep voice said.

Looking over his shoulder, Ciaran saw a tall man with red skin and black hair. His eyes were of a solid gold and the pupils were black slits. The large hand which rested on his shoulder was human enough, but the fingernails were more like claws, their black color glistening like wet paint. The strange man towered over Ciaran, standing more than two feet higher than him. Ciaran had never seen a man as tall in his life. He stepped away, frightened.

"I apologize if I have startled you. There is nothing for you to fear my friend. You must be hungry. Please, come with me. I have prepared food for you to restore your strength."

"Who are you?"

"I am the lord of this castle. My name is Avot, and I am the dragon of this mountain."

Ciaran paused, studying the dragon's face. Avot smiled down at him, then started to walk towards the door in the center of the right wall. Once he was eight paces away, Ciaran hurried to catch up, not wanting to seem rude. He matched the dragon's stride, which was long but slow. Avots pace gave Ciaran the impression that the dragon wasn't in too much of a hurry. Neither of them spoke as they crossed the large room to the door. Avot waved his hand and the door opened for him. There were no servants behind it, which made Ciaran curious if he had managed it with some magic. It was clear to him that there was a great deal more to learn about dragons than he had ever supposed.

When they entered the next room, Ciaran was amazed to find himself in a feasting hall filled with long wooden tables and benches. Golden plates and crystal goblets were set out, but there was no food in the center of the tables. Instead, there was a long piece of cloth that ran down the center, the purple fabric shimmering from the light of the two enormous chandeliers which hung from the ceiling. On the opposite side of the feast hall, a long high table was set out, positioned perpendicular to the center tables. It was set on a platform which was raised up above the rest of the room by three feet and two steps had been built on either side to allow easy access. The high table had nine chairs instead of benches and they were placed only on the far side. Ciaran looked at the middle most chair which was made from solid gold and designed in a manner that was so intricate, he found himself pausing to admire it. The chair was made of hundreds of interwoven threads of gold that meshed together in fifty different patterns. Beneath the gold, he could see sections of wood which must have made up the base. The back was upholstered with a thick comfortable looking cushion that was covered in deep red fabric and embroidered with the head of a dragon.

Once again, Ciaran had to hurry to catch up to Avot, who had continued walking while Ciaran had paused to admire the dining throne. Walking alongside the dragon, he followed Avot to the right stairs and ascended to the platform. He looked at the table and saw that a small chair had been set out beside the throne. It was unoccupied, but seemed just the right size for a goblin. Feeling guilty that in his astonishment and admiration, he'd forgotten about his friend, Ciaran turned to Avot to ask where he was.

"Your friend is still resting," Avot answered, as if the dragon could hear the thoughts of his mind.

Unsettled, Ciaran nodded. "He likes cheese."

"That he does. Based on how much he has already eaten, I would say he loves it. I still have a hard time understanding how a fellow of his size could devour so much in a single sitting." Avot let out a deep laugh. "Come, take a seat."

The dragon sat on his throne and Ciaran sat down in the chair to the left. It was soft and comfortable, the wooden arms also set with upholstered cushions. Sinking down into the chair, he felt like he could sit there for the rest of his life.

"What foods do you desire, my friend?"

Ciaran's stomach rumbled and his thoughts turned to roasted pork, honeycomb, and fresh bread. As these thoughts entered his mind, the doors on both sides of the platform, which Ciaran had failed to originally notice, and eight servants walked out. They carried silver platters of food, and two of them carried one which had an entire roasted pig. The food was set out before them and a servant began to fill Ciaran's plate. Working quickly, the servants finished filling Avot's plate as well, then with a bow, they retreated. Ciaran watched them as they went. Each was human in form, but their skin tones were either shades of blue, red, or yellow. They all had the same eyes as their master, but they were not nearly as tall.

Are they dragons too? Ciaran wondered.

"Eat, and then I will answer your questions. You seem to have many."

Ciaran nodded, but still waited for the dragon to be the first to take a bite of his food. It was a custom for Ciaran, one he wasn't certain the dragon would follow, but he felt a need to be polite. Avot reached down, took a slice of pork, and then swallowed it whole. Relieved,

Ciaran took up the dining knife and spoon, then started to eat. No matter what he ate, it was the most flavorful and perfectly prepared thing Ciaran had ever tasted. The pork was salted, the meat still juicy, and most of all warm. His bread was crisp on the outside, but soft and fluffy within. When he smeared the portion of honey atop it, the warm bread made the honey melt. He tried to slow down his eating, but he was famished. When he finished his first plate, he was still hungry. He glanced at the food but did not reach for it. Ciaran did not want to appear rude.

Avot reached out, and began to place more food on Ciaran's plate, this time adding new dishes of roasted vegetables, cakes, and fish.

"Please, eat your fill. There is plenty, so enjoy as much as you would like."

Ciaran thanked his host, and started to eat the food Avot had added to his plate. The dragon had just as large an appetite and finished three plates in the time that it took Ciaran to finish his second. Still hungry, Ciaran took the initiative and reached for more food, determined to taste a bit of everything he had not yet tried.

To his surprise, Ciaran did not feel full until all of the food that had been laid out on the table was gone. Spooning the last bite of a pudding into his mouth, he savored it. Then, leaning back in his chair, he let out a sigh. Two servants returned, and filled the crystal goblets with warm cider. Reaching out, he took the goblet, and drank. The spiced cider relaxed him and Ciaran couldn't help but smile.

"Thank you for such wonderful food and for your hospitality," Ciaran said.

"You are welcome."

"I must also apologize since I feel as though I have come uninvited to your doorstep."

"Nonsense. All who visit are, in one way or another, both uninvited and welcome. Though, I am surprised that you managed to come at all. Humans do not typically come through the passage you took."

"Well, I thank you again. I do not know how to repay your generosity."

"What was given to you Ciaran was a gift, not intended to be repaid. You and your goblin friend owe me nothing. But I am interested to know why you have taken the effort to journey here. Zict was silent on the matter, and told me that he was just a guide for you. So tell me, Ciaran, why have you come to speak with me?"

"Did Zict also leave out the fact that he encouraged me to come?"

"That he did."

"Well, he encouraged me to come and speak with you so I could better understand your motives. I came because I wanted to understand why you set fire to the Temple of Umris in my home city of Umrithos."

"Ah, that is an interesting question. Tell me, do you believe that I did so without cause?"

"No. I believe you had cause or at least a reason."

"Interesting. Permit me another question. Do you believe that I am not an admirer of art?"

"No. I believe that you must love art. Otherwise, you would not make everything in your palace beautiful. Even the simple things look like they were made with care by masterful hands."

"You are correct. I do admire art."

Ciaran felt a little irritated that the dragon was avoiding his question. "If you are such an admirer of art, why did you set the temple on fire?"

Avot smiled. "I went because it was requested of me. I too am a humble follower of the Gods and Goddesses. My devotion to serving them, no matter the strangeness of their requests, is absolute."

"So Umris asked you to set fire to her own temple?"

"The destruction of the temple was not the point. She knew that a little loss would motivate your people into action."

"Why would we need that? All my life, I have only known my people to be busy and industrious. We have more artists now than ever."

"And yet, are they producing work that is uninspired or derivative of that which has come before. Certainly, there is more to be desired. Do you not agree?"

Ciaran thought about all of the beautiful paintings that had been destroyed. He did not think of them as uninspired or derivative. But he didn't think he knew better than Avot either. "I don't know if I understand enough of what you mean to answer your question."

"Come with me. Perhaps I can show you."

Avot rose and began to make his way back to the

entrance of the dining hall. Ciaran followed, his shoulders hunched forward, chin tucked towards his chest. When they entered the first hall, Avot paused, then placed his hand on Ciaran's shoulder. Lifting his head, he looked at Avot whose attention was on the far wall where the moving dragon was projected.

"What do you think of this?"

"It is the single greatest piece of art I have ever seen."

"Why?"

"I have never seen anything like it before. The colors are so perfect, the way the gemstones in the throne catch the light. It shouldn't be possible. Who made it?"

"I did."

"How?"

"Years upon years of experimenting with light and gemstones. At first it was created by accident. But over time, I learned how to set the lights and stones so they would do what I wished." Avot released Ciaran's shoulder, then started towards the door on the opposite side of the large throne room. "Come, there is still much to see."

Crossing the room, they reached the door and with a wave of his hand, Avot caused it to open. They strode through, entering a long hallway that was filled with tapestries. Each tapestry depicted a dragon. Though similar, each dragon's scales were a different combination of colors and the horns on their heads formed distinct shapes. Between the tapestries were doors. They passed five sets of doors before stopping at one. This too, Avot opened with a wave of his hand. Entering, Ciaran was struck by the number of paintings which hung on the walls. Hundreds of paintings in golden frames covering every inch of the walls. The room was as large as a city block. Large chandeliers hung from the ceiling, providing excellent lighting that no painting was covered in shadow.

Avot led them to the back of the room where he stopped before a painting that held a striking resemblance to the masterpiece which had hung in the Temple of Umris. It depicted the Goddess with golden hair and dark eyes standing among the clouds with golden dragons on either side and satyrs worshiping at her feet. But this painting was so much more detailed than the one he remembered. Ciaran was awestruck as he looked at it. Avot said nothing, giving him time to admire the painting.

"This is not the same painting. Is it?" Ciaran asked.

"No. But it was made by the same artist."

"Which did he paint first?"

"He painted them together."

"I do not understand."

"When this painting was made, it was done after a true fire that had burned your city to the ground. That was before Umris was your patron Goddess and before Umrithos became a city devoted to the arts. Do you know that story?"

"Of course I do. Everyone knows the story of how Eamon won the favor of Umris with his painting and how she blessed our city so it could be rebuilt."

"Well, at the end of his life, he wanted to do one final painting. His sight was failing and his body was old making it difficult for him to hold a paintbrush. Deciding that it would be his final great effort, Eamon decided he would recreate his greatest painting, but bring every skill he'd learned in his life to the new version. This was his final masterpiece."

"It is beautiful."

"Indeed it is."

"But I don't understand why the original painting needed to be destroyed."

"Like I explained, Umris asked me to burn it to teach your city a lesson. She wanted you to understand that artists should never stop trying to learn something new, to make something better. But most importantly, that you can only learn so much by copying what previous generations of artists have done. All this time, you have been trying to copy Eamon's work, and it wasn't even his best."

"Could that lesson not be taught without destroying the paintings?"

"The Goddess didn't think so. Tell me this, Ciaran. Would you have ever come to my palace had I not set fire to the temple?"

"No."

"Why not?"

Ciaran paused, contemplating all of the events that had happened since the fire. Without it and the priestesses commission for new art, he wouldn't have had the opportunity to become an apprentice. If he had not become an apprentice, he would have never been sent out to find pigments for paint. And, if he had never met Zict, then he would have followed his original instructions and got the pigments from the places Master Edgar had instructed.

"Because I would have never had a need to go outside my city to look for painting pigments."

"I see. And why did you have to do that?"

"Well, every master artist in the city is trying to create a new painting for the temple, and my own master needed more paint. That is why I was sent out and had I not met Zict, I wouldn't have made it here either."

"Now I am beginning to understand a little more myself why Umris sent me the request. She wanted to see you grow as well as see the other artists grow. Now they have an opportunity to do so."

"I still think this could have happened without losing so much fine work to your fire."

"Perhaps. But even the greatest painting in that temple was not lost, not truly," Avot said, pointing back to the painting on the wall. "There are places where the lost art will be remembered. Even as we speak, they still exist in the galleries of the Goddess. As perfect as they day they were presented to her."

Ciaran smiled, a sense of relief flooding over him. He believed the dragon's word. Turning his attention back to the painting of Umris, he took a moment to study the excellence of the work. It was like he was seeing it for the first time. Ciaran understood more now about how the colors worked together and he could see so many shades represented. He was both inspired and daunted by the prospect of trying to paint such a thing. But he was inspired to work until he could do so. When he turned back to Avot, he saw that the dragon was standing by another painting, hands clasped behind his back.

"May I stay here for a while to look at the paintings?"

"Ciaran, you are welcome to stay here as long as you wish."

13
THE JOURNEY HOME

The first three days were used up in simple admiration. The fourth and fifth days were spent sketching. The sixth and seventh days were dedicated to painting. On the eighth day, when Ciaran woke up in the familiar soft bed at the top of the tower, he knew that it was past time for him to return home. He had already been away from home much longer than he'd expected and he didn't want his family to worry.

Ciaran didn't want to leave and he knew that he could happily spend the rest of his life here. Climbing out of bed, Ciaran went to the corner where his pack was sitting, and began to prepare it for the journey home. Everything was already prepared and without Ciaran asking, one of the servants had packed new food into his bag which had not been there the day before.

"So, it seems Avot knew I was going to be leaving before I did," Ciaran said to himself.

It was still strange how Avot seemed to know things. Ciaran wasn't sure if the dragon could read his mind or if there was some other magic involved. As much as he wanted to know the secret, Ciaran was fine leaving it a mystery. Sometimes there was more wonder in not knowing.

Once he was dressed in his traveling clothes, Ciaran put on his cloak which had been mended to repair the damage caused by the fire. The cloth was firmer now and there was light embroidery on the hood and hem which was done in a flame like pattern. The embroidery thread was a shade darker than the brown color of the cloak which helped make it blend in. Ciaran felt a sudden weight as he wondered how he was going to thank Avot for everything the dragon had done. Certainly, there was nothing he could give that could repay all that the dragon had given them. A deep sense of gratitude filled him and Ciaran was determined, at the very least, to express his sincerest thanks to Avot before departing.

Gathering his pack and artist's bag, Ciaran left the room and began to descend from the tower. He was used to the winding trip down to the bottom, and he felt a little sad that this would be his last time doing so. This didn't cause him to linger, but Ciaran found himself enjoying it more. Every time he passed a purple flamed torch hanging in a silver sconce, he enjoyed its simple beauty. When he descended the stairs from one landing to the next, he admired how perfectly each step had been placed. He ran his hand against the wall, the black stone smooth and warm to the touch. Reaching the bottom, he strolled out into the large throne room and looked at the glittering color projection of the flying dragon on the wall. It didn't seem to matter how many times Ciaran saw it. The projected image was just as wonderful as ever.

Glancing away from the image, Ciaran saw that Avot was sitting on his throne, his red and black tunic trimmed with gold. A crown had been set atop his head. Something Ciaran had never seen on the dragon before. It was shaped like two large dragon horns connected by a thick golden band. There were no jewels set into the crown, but the golden band had been worked so well that it had a glow. Sitting on the arm of the throne was Zict, who was holding a conversation with Avot, the goblins small hands moving as he spoke. The two of them noticed Ciaran and stopped their conversation.

"Ciaran," Avot called, "come, join us."

Obeying the dragon, he walked over to the throne and bowed his head. "I don't know how to thank you for your generous hospitality."

"Your company over the last week has been more than enough recompense. However, your gratitude is also very much appreciated. "

Zict bounded off the arm of the throne and landed on Ciaran's shoulder. The goblin gripped the cloak and the familiar pinch of the claws made Ciaran feel ready.

"I appreciate that you have also prepared food for my journey home."

"My pleasure, though, it appears you may not need all of

it. Zict has convinced me to fly you back to the edge of the forest by your home. You've been out for far too long and I am certain your family is worried about you."

Ciaran felt a wave of excitement flow through him. "That would be an honor."

"There used to be a time when humans would ride dragons, though it was long before my hatching. I am quite curious to give it a try." Avot stood and as he pulled back his shoulders, Ciaran thought he was even taller than he'd been before. "Are you ready to depart?"

"Yes."

"Then follow me."

Avot strode towards the door which led to the rooms and galleries. Ciaran looked longingly at the closed doors, making a silent wish that he could return.

"You are always welcome to return here, Ciaran. I hope... no, I expect a visit from time to time."

"It will be an honor. You can be certain I will return as often as my circumstances permit."

"Just be sure to use the back entrance next time," Avot said as they reached the end of the hall.

He waved his hand and the massive door opened revealing a short staircase that ended at a large tunnel. They descended the steps and Ciaran looked over his shoulder at the palace. The walls were high and there were spiked stone pillars on the corners. He could see part of the large tower and then the hole in the mountain with the glowing obsidian walls. Turning his attention to the tunnel, he hurried to catch up with the dragon who had continued walking while Ciaran had paused in admiration.

Matching the dragon's stride, they continued through the tunnel which was growing darker by the moment. The three of them didn't speak as they walked and Ciaran was content with the silence. The tunnel had a gentle incline that went on for several miles. The walls and ceiling were not carved and for the most part had the rough look of a natural formation. Even so, the size of the tunnel was consistent, never growing larger or narrower as they went. Judging by their walking pace, Ciaran figured they had walked just over three miles when they reached the end of the cave. The wall at the entrance was made from the same black stone as the palace. The door was large enough for a full size dragon to walk through and it opened for them with a wave of Avot's hand. It moved slowly, grinding on the ground, sending a rumbling sound back through the tunnel. Brilliant daylight spilled in and Ciaran found it difficult to keep his eyes open.

The sound of tweeting birds and rustling leaves were a welcome relief to Ciaran. Fresh scents of grass and flowers drifted in and he took in a deep breath which was sweeter than any he could remember. Ciaran no longer felt as loathsome about leaving the dragon's palace and forcing his eyes open, he walked out into the sunshine. As the light bathed his face, he felt warm and fresh and new. Zict let out a similar sigh and made a chirping noise. Avot continued walking and with every step, he seemed to grow a bit taller. When he was twenty paces away, he shook his head and his human features began to disappear, growing more angular as his nose and mouth began to extend. Every part of his body began to shift, grow, and distort as they transformed from human to dragon. Clothes became scales, the crown became horns, and within a few heartbeats, a mighty red dragon was standing on the mountain foothill. Ciaran noticed that Avot's large body cast a long shadow.

Ciaran admired the dragon and noticed that the scales were larger than dinner platters. There was so much detail and texture to them, and light seemed to be absorbed rather than reflected. He didn't look glossy like a serpent might have, but that didn't take away from his appearance. Instead, he felt like it had been enhanced. Avot lowered his head and rested it on the ground.

"Climb onto my neck and find a place near the top of my head." Avot's voice was deep and it caused Ciaran's entire body to vibrate.

Walking to the dragon, he used the spikes that grew on the dragon's jaw like ladder steps and climbed onto the top of the neck. There was enough space between the spines that he could sit comfortably, and the spike just at the crown of the dragon's head curled forward slightly. He wrapped his arms around it and held his hands tightly together. His stomach fluttered as Avot lifted his head and Ciaran did his best not to cry out. Zict let out a yelp of his own.

"Do not be afraid," Avot said. "I will move slowly so you do not fall."

The dragon turned about and with his enormous tail,

closed the doors to his tunnel. Ciaran took a moment to examine the mountain and surrounding hillsides so he could remember them when it came time to return. The dragon began to climb the mountain, moving up the steep inclines and cliffs with ease. At times, he would use his wings, like additional limbs, to help him climb. Ciaran was surprised how quickly he grew accustomed to the dragon's movements. It wasn't unlike riding a horse, but he didn't feel the need to shift his weight. When they reached the top of the mountain, Ciaran looked down the hole at the fire which burned across the cracked black stones. They looked so small from their vantage, and Ciaran noticed that they were arranged in a spiral pattern that looked like a dragon curled inside an egg. He smiled, and memorized the sight so he could draw it later.

"Are you two ready?" Avot asked as he walked to the edge of the peak.

"I am ready," Ciaran said, unable to keep the tremor from his voice.

Avot stretched out his wings, flapped them three times and leapt off the cliff. Ciaran closed his eyes, clutched the spike, and clenched his jaw. His stomach lurched and tickled. Then all was still, like he was floating in a pool. Feeling the wind cool his face, Ciaran enjoyed the way it moved his hair and fluttered his eyelids. It took him a moment before he felt brave enough to open his eyes, and when he did, he gasped.

They flew well above the rolling hills and rivers below, and it was as if he were standing atop a tall mountain.

Ciaran could see for miles and miles, but they flew fast which allowed him to see with greater detail the land as they went. The longer he looked, the more amazed he became. As they flew over a stream, he caught a glimpse of several deer who had paused to take a drink. Two doe's were standing near a stag whose large horns had a wet sheen to them. Passing by the deer, they continued soaring over the hills and reached the beginnings of a wood. All this was new, the land on the opposite sides of the mountains and valleys, where Ciaran had traveled before. It was interesting how different the vegetation and landscape was. While there were similarities to what he had seen during his travels, the land below them now was greener and more densely packed with shrubs and smaller trees rather than filled with forest or rolling hills. Ciaran wondered why either side of the mountains would be so different. Flying over a wetland, he admired the way the water rose up between thick bushes and scraggly trees. The dragon's body was reflected in the water, but only looked like a black and red smudge.

Avot flapped his wings, and they lurched upwards. Ciaran felt his stomach flutter again, and then all went calm as the dragon stretched out his large wings. The air was colder now and he felt like he needed to breathe more frequently. Hunching forward, Ciaran laid as much of his body against the dragon's scales as he could and was warmed by it.

"How are you both fairing?" Avot asked, his voice rumbling through Ciaran's entire body.

"A bit cold is all," Ciaran said.

"Then we shall go lower once again."

Pulling in his wings, Avot shifted his head, and then they began a sharp dive towards the ground. Heart thumping in his chest, Ciaran felt his stomach lurch worse than any of the times before. He couldn't help but close his eyes. Then all was well again. He enjoyed the feeling for a moment before he felt brave enough to open his eyes. Ciaran saw that they were soaring well above the wetlands, but he was now much warmer and breathing was easier.

"What do you think of flying?"

"It's wonderful," Zict answered.

"What about you, Ciaran? What do you think?"

"I can not explain how something can both delight and terrify me to such extreme degrees at the same time. It is a joy, but my body and my heart don't always feel it."

"Well, I shall try to keep our flight as steady as possible so that you may enjoy it."

True to his word, Avot continued and kept their flight steady with more gentle flaps of his wings. Ciaran relaxed and found delight more in the observation of the land than in the sensations of flying. He was beginning to grow a little envious of the dragon, wishing that he too could fly. Ciaran wondered how much of the world he could see if he too could take to the sky like a dragon and travel so swiftly across land. His envy didn't last long, his mind occupied with awe and appreciation of what he was presently witnessing. Something had changed inside Ciaran over the short weeks of his journey. He realized that he now saw things with additional clarity because he was better at paying attention. Colors stood out to him and he was amazed at how light and shadow would make so much out of a single leaf. All he had done before to try and capture what he saw had been missing that understanding. Then, Ciaran perceived an even more profound change within himself. A type of excitement and wonder that had laid dormant. He genuinely felt inspired by the world around him and happy to be alive.

Ciaran could feel a change in the way the wind struck his face as the dragon slowed his flight. Then, in gentle descent, they landed upon the ground in the middle of a glade. The yellow grass swayed gently back and forth as Avot beat his wings for the last time. Leaning forward, Avot laid his head down upon the ground and Ciaran climbed back down, once again using the spikes on the dragon's jaw like a ladder.

Finding the ground to be both steady and secure, Ciaran released the last bit of tension from his shoulders. His stomach also relaxed and he took a deep breath. He looked at Avot and glanced into one of his large golden eyes. It had a glow to it which illuminated the red scales of his brow and cheek.

"Avot, thank you so much for taking us home."

"Of course. It has been so long since I have had the pleasure of making new friends. Your company was welcome and your eventual return to my palace is eagerly anticipated."

"Before we go, may I ask one final favor?"

"Of course."

"Will you let me take an hour or two to draw you?"

Avot rose up, then nodded his enormous dragon head. "It would be an honor."

Ciaran walked a ways away, then sitting down upon the grass, he took out his sketchbook and silverpoint pencil. He flipped through the sketchbook, amazed at how many pages he had already filled with drawings or watercolor paintings. Turning to one of the final pages, he looked up and began to draw. Avot's posture had changed and the dragon stood tall, his wings folded in, but stretched out enough that they looked large and strong.

The first few sketches were done to capture the proportions of the dragon, Ciaran's focus being more on the shape than the detail. Then, he did a drawing of the dragon's face and eye, making sure he shaded in the details of how the light shone from both the sun and the eye. On the final page, he did a full drawing that was as detailed as it could be for the size. Smiling down, Ciaran now had his reference. He would paint Avot the Dragon and present it to the Goddess. Ciaran was certain Master Edgar wouldn't mind. He would do it on his own time.

"Thank you for everything," Ciaran said, closing his sketchbook. "I look forward to our next meeting."

"As do I. Farewell my friends."

Without another word, Avot jumped into the sky, the strong beating of his wings causing the wind to ruffle Ciaran's hair. He watched until the dragon disappeared into the clouds. Then, he packed away his sketchbook and started towards home.

❧ 14 ❧
THE UNBELIEVABLE STORY

When Ciaran emerged from the wood, he saw that he was just north of the city of Umrithos. Zict had been uncharacteristically quiet during their walk, and had fidgeted back and forth like he was fighting a fit of anxiety. Looking at the goblin, Ciaran saw that his friend's ears were drawn back so they laid almost flat against his head and his eyes were little more than narrow slits.

"Is everything well?" Ciaran asked.

Zict shook his head, but said nothing to elaborate upon the issue.

"What is wrong? Is there something I can do to help?"

Zict started to shake his head, then stopped. He opened his eyes a little more, then tucked his head down so his chin was resting against his chest. Then, in a soft trembling voice, he said, "I don't want to say goodbye."

"Neither do I, my friend. If it could be, I would that you

would remain on my shoulder talking sense into my ear for the rest of time."

"I would like that too."

Ciaran paused, then smiled. "Then why are you sad? I see no reason why you could not remain with me if you wished for it. Unless you must return home."

Zict's ears perked up and he smiled. "So, I can stay with you. I thought you said your mother would not approve."

"I know that's what I said. If you really would wish to come home with me, I would love to have you. Now, we might have to talk mother into seeing reason. She might be a little startled at first to have a goblin in the house, but I'm certain she will not object once she meets you."

"I...I would like that very much."

"Will they not miss you at your home?" Ciaran asked.

"There is no home to miss me. The truth is, I am not as well suited for goblin life as you might think. They say I am too fascinated with humans for my own good. I am no more at home when I am with them than I am wandering the countryside."

"Well then, let us go on to the city and I will show you your new home. A home where you will always be welcome and where cheese is abundant."

"Now, that is the most sensible thing you have ever said."

The front door to his home was locked when he arrived. The sun was low in the sky and it was perhaps an hour before supper. Ciaran's stomach grumbled and though he had food in his pack, the thought of eating his mothers stew with fresh bread was too appetizing to spoil. He knocked on the door, then took a step back. Zict sat on his shoulder, the goblin still as a statue. Ciaran heard sounds from within his home, and then the scraping of the lock bolt as it was drawn back. The door opened, and his mother greeted him with a wide smile.

"Ciaran!" she said, tears welling in her eyes.

Stumbling forward, he gave his mother a big hug. She held him tight for a bit longer than he would have wanted, but he allowed it anyway. When she finally pulled away, she ruffled his hair and then gripped his shoulders.

"You stink. Go, take a bath. Supper will be ready when you are done."

Just as she turned to walk away, his mother paused, then her eyes went wide. She noticed Zict who was still sitting on his shoulder. Ciaran smiled and then lifted his hand so his friend could climb onto it. Once Zict was secure on his palm, Ciaran lifted him up so his mother could be introduced.

"Mother, this is my friend Zict. He helped me while I was away. Zict doesn't have a home and I invited him to stay with us."

At first, his mother didn't say anything. After a minute, she managed to put on a smile, though her shock hadn't faded. Then, she gave Zict a nod.

"Well, any friend of Ciaran's is a friend of mine. You are more than welcome to stay. Remind me, your name is?"

"Zict. And it is a pleasure to meet you."

Springing forward, Zict leapt onto his mothers shoulder. Ciaran felt an immediate panic as he saw the smile fade from his mothers face.

"Please, let me be of assistance. I am considered quite a chef where I come from. Perhaps I may help you prepare supper as Ciaran gets himself ready."

Ciaran smiled at his mother and gave her a nod. She took a breath, then they all went inside. Zict leapt from his mothers shoulder to the table and then bounded to the fireplace where several loaves of bread were baking. Sparing one glance at his mother, who had gone back to the stew, Ciaran went up the stairs to his room so he could unpack.

Once inside his room, he dropped his pack in the corner and then set the artist bag on his desk. He took a moment to look at his old paintings which hung on the wall. They didn't have the same color and allure they once had. Still, he smiled at them. They were reminders of who he had been and what he had been capable of. Reminders and mementos of a captured moment in time. For that reason alone he found them valuable, though they were not masterpieces anyone else might value. Looking at the blank canvas that had been set out on an easel in the corner, Ciaran felt excitement at the prospect of starting his very own painting. But that would have to wait.

Ciaran took fresh clothes down to the bath, and made quick work of cleaning himself. The bathwater was cold which made the washing unpleasant. As he rinsed the soap and dirt from his hair, he was amazed at how dirty he was. With a shiver, he toweled off and got dressed. The fresh clothes still had the scents of the soaps used during the laundering, and he felt warm in them. Returning to the kitchen, he was surprised to find his mother and father both standing at the dinner table laughing.

Zict was leaping about, a spoon in his hand, describing some elaborate fight. Ciaran moved closer to watch.

"...then, charging on the backs of lizards, we rushed down the hill to battle. Goblin against gnome. I knocked free dozens of their silly red hats and in the end, the gnomes rode away on their rabbits in shame."

As Zict finished his story, he thrust his spoon into the air with a triumphant call, and then bowed his head. Ciaran chuckled and joined his parents in clapping. His father looked over at him, seeming to take notice of Ciaran's arrival for the first time.

"You truly have made such an interesting friend, my boy."

"He certainly made my journey a whole lot easier."

"Come, let us sit down and eat," mother said. "We can finish our conversation and enjoy the food while it is still warm."

Ciaran took his seat on the side of the table closest to the fire. Zict strolled over and sat beside a small dining saucer his mother had set out for him. The goblin set his fingers on the edge of the saucer, looking down at the small bread and cup of soup laid out for him. Ciaran's father offered a quick gesture of thanks to the Goddess, then took a bite.

"This is wonderful, my dear," he said.

Ciaran looked over at his mother who also made a gesture of thanks and took a small bite of her soup. Then both of his parents looked at him. He did the same gesture, lifting his hand with the palm up, fingers extended like he was holding a bowl, then muttered a small thanks. He ate his first bite of the soup and the warmth immediately spread through him, banishing the rest of the cold that had come over him during the bath. Without another word, they all started to eat. Zict joined in, giving Ciaran a look of confusion.

"It's just a custom," he whispered. "An offer of thanks to the Goddess for another meal."

"And for Ciaran's safe return," his mother added.

"Then we should be thanking the dragon as well," Zict said, raising his hand which was clutching a small chunk of bread. "To the Goddess and the dragon!"

"Tell us, Ciaran, what is your friend speaking of?"

"It's a long story. I should probably start at the beginning. Did Zict already tell you how we met?"

"Briefly," his father said. "He mentioned that you two came across each other on the road and that you helped him escape the wrath of a vengeful serpent."

"True enough. Though the vengeful serpent part might be a bit of an exaggeration."

"I wasn't embellishing," Zict said. "I think I would know more about what makes him vengeful than you do, Ciaran."

"I won't argue with you then."

"So. Tell us more about this dragon," his mother said, her voice sharp with concern.

"Our journey ended with the dragon. Let me explain how we got there."

Ciaran told his parents with as much detail as he could remember, the experiences of his journey. Zict proved to be an excellent storytelling companion who would cut in and add additional details Ciaran either forgot or had failed to mention. Shortly after starting his story, Ciaran ran up to his room and retrieved his sketchbook. This made the story easier to tell as he flipped through the drawings and explained the experiences behind them. The story continued past dinner and well into the evening. Both of his parents were quiet, asking only a question here or there. Ciaran couldn't tell if they believed him or not. When he fished explaining how Avot had flown them back, he went silent, waiting for a rebuke. It didn't come.

Quiet, his father got up from the table, then walked to the pantry where he retrieved a bottle of wine and fig cakes. He set them down on the table, and then removed the cork from the bottle. Pouring the wine into his mothers cup first, his father then filled his own. Ciaran watched him, uncertainty filling him as the house continued to be quiet.

"That is quite an adventure, my boy. Almost unbelievable at times."

"I know."

"I would caution you not to tell this story to other

people. Especially where the dragon is involved. Most will not understand."

"You don't have to tell me that, father. I know. I was afraid of the dragon myself before meeting him. I won't be spreading my story around."

"We are happy you are home," his mother said. "And, we are happy to hear that you had such a wonderful adventure."

"Zict," his father said, pointing down at the plate of fig cakes, "have you ever eaten one of these?"

"No. But I am very eager to give them a try."

"Let's enjoy them and celebrate my son's triumphant return. He left the city as a boy, and returned an artist."

Ciaran sat up a little straighter in his chair and smiled.

For the first time in his life, he felt like his father was proud of the idea he wanted to be an artist. His father winked at him and then snagged a fig cake from off the plate. They ate and joked and laughed. As the sun was starting to set, Ciaran helped his mother clear the dinner table while his father retired to a rocking chair beside the fire. He took out his pipe and began to fill it from his pouch. Zict joined his father and began to inquire about the pipe. As they spoke, Ciaran took his sketchbook, and went to the door.

"Where do you think you are off to?" his mother said.

"Just going to visit Maeve."

"Take a cake with you then."

Ciaran returned to the table and his mother handed him a fresh cloth which he used to wrap two fig cakes. She gave him a kiss on the cheek, then shooed him away.

"I'll be back soon, Zict," Ciaran called. "Keep father company, will you?"

"Yes, yes, no need to rush. Take your time."

"Just be back before night," his mother said.

"I will."

Rushing out the door, he leapt from the top of the steps to the road, then hurried down to the end of the street. When Ciaran arrived at Maeve's house, he glanced up at the sky and saw that the sun was just a knuckle above the horizon. That meant he had about fifteen minutes before sunset which would give him enough time to run home before it was dark. Not wanting to waste any more time, he knocked on the door and waited.

Maeve's father answered. The top of his head was bald but the sides still had dark red hair which was trimmed short. His grumpy expression changed when he saw Ciaran.

"Good evening," Ciaran said with a bob of his head.

"Good to see you, Ciaran. One moment, I will go and fetch Maeve."

"Thank you."

Without another word, he left and Ciaran remained at the door, awkwardly shifting back and forth. He heard Maeve's footsteps before she arrived. When she darted out of the door, she had a huge smile on her face and her red hair bounced. She bounded forward and gave him a hug which caused Ciaran to take a step back in order to keep his balance. With the sketchbook in one hand and the cakes in another, he felt just a little awkward. Maeve pulled back and looked him up and down.

“Looks like you returned in one piece.”

“I did.”

“You look like you ate rather well.”

“Are you calling me plump?”

“Not at all,” she said, eyeing the cloth covered cakes in his hand. “What are those?”

“Fig cakes.” Ciaran unwrapped them and then held them out.

Maeve took a cake, leaving the second for him. They sat down on the steps before her house and began to eat the cakes. Ciaran was full, but he didn’t have a hard time making room for just one more of the sweets.

“What’s that?” Maeve asked, gesturing to his sketchbook.

“They are the drawings I made during my journey. Want to see them?”

“Of course.”

Shoving the rest of the fig cake into his mouth, Ciaran wiped his fingers clean on the cloth, then unwrapped the leather cord which held his sketchbook closed. He then opened it and began to turn the pages.

“These are wonderful. Did you actually see these things?”

“Ya. Every single one.”

Maeve finished her cake, and then Ciaran passed her the sketchbook so she could thumb through it at her own speed. She moved through the pages quickly, eager to see them all rather than linger her attention on any single drawing or painting. When she reached the end, she stopped abruptly, her eyes going wide.

"This is the dragon? You saw him?"

"I did."

"And he let you sketch him?"

"Obviously," Ciaran said. He wanted to share the whole story with her, but there wasn't enough time tonight, and he remembered his fathers warning.

"Are you still going to try and paint him?"

"I'll try my best."

"I can't wait to see it."

"I promise that you will be the first person who gets to."

"Are you going to present it?"

"I'm not a master artist yet. Besides, I don't think the priestess would appreciate such a submission."

"That's not a good reason not to."

"Still, even if I did submit it, I won't win."

"Why does that matter?"

Ciaran shrugged. "I guess it doesn't."

"Promise me then that you will present it."

"What if it is not good enough?"

Maeve raised an eyebrow and tilted her head. "Ciaran."

"Fine. I will present it."

"Good."

"Tomorrow, when I get home from working with Master Edgar, I have a new friend you need to meet."

"Who is this new friend?"

"You will see."

"Oh, don't do that. You have to tell me."

"No. It's better that it be a surprise."

"You are the worst sometimes, Ciaran."

"I know."

"Can I keep this overnight?" Maeve said, holding up the sketchbook. "I'd like to look at the drawings some more."

"Of course. I'd love to know what you think of it all."

The two of them sat together for a few minutes as the sun started to set. They looked at the drawings some more and Ciaran told the story of how the spider had taught him how to draw a web. She laughed as he told it, seeming completely delighted by the whole idea of spiders making art. When the sun disappeared below the horizon, Ciaran gave Maeve a hug goodbye, then rushed home. Though tired and ready to turn in for the night, he had a strange feeling of excitement. He was looking forward to tomorrow with more anticipation than any day he could remember. He was finally going to be an artist's apprentice and he was going to start his painting of the dragon.

15
THE MASTER'S PAINTING

Strolling through the streets, Ciaran felt like things were dull and that he was out of place. The excitement the fire had caused before he'd left was gone and the streets were filled with the normal humdrum of life. He caught a glimpse of the temple and was astonished to see that the roof was covered with tarps and new lumber had been stacked near the front. Wrapping the stone building were frameworks of wooden poles and boards. He could see men hoisting stones or large beams with ropes and pulleys. Ciaran wondered how much of the rebuilding would be completed before the festival. They had already made a great deal more progress than he'd expected, but it still didn't seem like it would be enough.

Filled with an even greater sense of urgency, Ciaran pulled on the strap of the artist's bag and hurried his way towards Master Edgar's studio. When he reached the block of large studio buildings, he saw that many of the apprentices were out and about, most of their green tunics stained with paint. He looked down at himself, his brown clothing and worn boots and shrugged. To his surprise, he no longer imagined himself wearing the clothes of an apprentice. He realized now that it didn't matter. Standing up just a little straighter, he made his way down the street and for the most part, ignored the others.

When he reached the end of the block, Ciaran did spare a glance at the large studio that belonged to Mistress Deirdre. He saw Declan through the window of the second story. The older boy was looking out and Ciaran waved to him. The gesture wasn't returned and in the next moment, Declan disappeared from view. Letting his hand fall to his side, Ciaran continued on his way, walking past the bakery, and down the street towards his master's home.

Nothing about the exterior appearance had changed, but Ciaran felt like he was looking at the building for the first time. The weathered bricks and peeling red door struck Ciaran as so mundane.

Perhaps the pristineness of Avot's palace has distorted my perception, Ciaran thought.

Still, as he approached, he couldn't help but feel like the building was missing something. It should have been built to look nicer. The materials were quality, but Ciaran found that the care within which they had been placed was missing. Like the builder had not cared about the project. Ciaran realized that it was very unlikely that Master Edgar had built the house, so it was unreasonable for him to expect it would have been done with the care a master painter would apply to their work. Still, it bothered him. The peeling red paint on the door bothered him even more. This, he knew that Master Edgar had control over, and wondered why his master hadn't bothered with it. His mind compared it to the care that had been put into every detail of Avot's palace. The contrast made Ciaran feel a bit uncomfortable. Until that moment, he would never have been able to explain it. But now, he knew that his attention to detail needed to extend beyond that of his work. Ciaran wasn't sure why it suddenly mattered to him. The quality of the building wouldn't have any impact on the finished paintings. Or at least, he didn't suspect it would.

Shaking his head, he pushed away the thoughts and walked up to the door. He knocked, then took a step back. Ciaran waited for several minutes, his arms folded in front of him, and when no one answered, he knocked again. Once more he waited, this time staying closer to the door so he could listen for footsteps. He heard nothing and after another five minutes, Ciaran grew irritated. He pounded on the door five times, using his fist to make the loudest sound he could. This time, when he took a step back from the door, he folded his arms.

When the door opened, it did so by just a sliver. Through it, Ciaran could see the old wrinkled face of Master Edgar. The old man was snarling and he pulled the door open just a bit more. His face softened, his anger replaced by astonishment. With wide eyes surrounded by wrinkles, Master Edgar let his mouth hang open.

"Do I know you?"

Ciaran wasn't certain how to answer. At that moment, he froze and took a step back.

"Why have you come to bother me! I don't like unexpected visitors."

"I am your apprentice. Remember? You took me on the day after the fire."

Master Edgar smiled wide and gave Ciaran a wink. "Sorry, I couldn't help myself."

Ciaran didn't laugh.

"What took you so long?"

"It really hasn't been that long. I was gone for two weeks. Certainly, you didn't expect me to get all the pigments in a day."

Master Edgar let out a laugh. "I suppose not. Come on in. I'm anxious to start mixing those new paints."

Retreating back inside, Master Edgar left the door open. Ciaran entered, let out a little irritated sigh and closed the door. Following the master down the dark hall, past the curtain, and into the studio, Ciaran found he felt the same distaste for the disarray inside the studio as he had felt about the outside. But all of that faded when he saw the magnificent canvas that sat half painted in the middle of the studio. No longer brown and dark red, the top half of the canvas was now covered with shades of blue and white, the beginnings of a magnificent sky. Yellows and greens covered other sections and though the painting was missing detail, the basic foundation of color brought a smile to Ciaran's face.

"Now, let's take a look at those pigments you brought me. They better be the right ones."

Ciaran had hardly removed the bag when Master Edgar snatched it and took it to a nearby table. This one had been moved since Ciaran's last visit, and a portion of it had been cleared. Other jars, bottles, and boxes had been set out around the edges leaving the center free for Master Edgar to work. Joining the old man, he watched in silence as he removed each of the jars. There was something different about them and Ciaran felt a pit in his stomach. Once all six of the jars were set out, Master Edgar began to remove the caps. The first one he opened was the jar of white pigment. He broke the seal which had been partially spun by the Moonweavers, not seeming to notice it. When his master looked inside, he let out a strange whistle of delight.

"What a pure color. I see that you followed my instructions for this one well enough." Master Edgar moved to the next jar and opened it. "And again with the yellow."

He opened them all, one by one, exclaiming his delight with them all. Once he was done, he turned around and looked at Ciaran, a wide grin on his face.

"You surprised me boy. I don't think I have ever seen such fine colored pigments in my life. You truly have proven yourself worthy to be an apprentice after all."

"Thank you," Ciaran said, bowing.

"Come on over, let me show you how to mix these into proper paints."

Without hesitation, Ciaran joined Master Edgar at the table. Master Edgar handed him a stone mortar and pestle, and poured linseed oil into the base. Then, taking a clean spoon, his master added in some of the white pigment.

"Grind these together boy, we want the paint to be smooth and thick."

Ciaran used the mortar to slowly grind the paint together and he was delighted as it began to form. Bit by bit, Master Edgar would add either oil or pigment to his mixture until satisfied with the result. Once the white paint was made, Ciaran transferred it into another bowl, then set to work mixing the next color. As he worked, Ciaran smiled. He couldn't wait to see what could be done with such perfect colored paint.

For eight weeks, Ciaran followed the same schedule. He would wake at dawn, eat a hearty breakfast with his family and Zict, then depart to Master Edgar's studio where he would work all day. He would return home for supper and then retire to his room where Ciaran would put himself to work on his own painting. Everything that he was learning from observing the painting techniques employed by Master Edgar had assisted him greatly and Ciaran's own dragon painting was taking form. He had started to base the painting off his sketch, but had quickly decided instead that the most majestic way to depict Avot would be in flight.

Ciaran had worked as diligently and carefully as possible, giving several layers time to dry as he worked. It was a slow process, but he didn't truly seem to notice. Instead, he enjoyed watching the slow progress as night by night, his painting began to take shape. During those eight weeks, Ciaran was happier than he ever remembered being. When the first day of the ninth week started, what had felt like a dream finally ended and Ciaran was faced with the reality that he was going to need to finish his painting. The thought of finishing frightened him, made his heart feel heavy, and all that day, his mind worried.

Master Edgar set him about the usual tasks when he arrived, and once he was done, he returned to the main studio where he sat on a stool, ready to prepare and mix any color requested. The great canvas which had been his master's work had developed into one of the most breath-taking landscape paintings Ciaran had ever seen. It looked like it belonged in the galleries of Avot's palace. The sky was half thunderhead, half bright white cumulous. The city of Umrithos was depicted, with large city walls and the temple that sat atop the hill, half of it cast in the shadow of the storm. Every detail, every color, was so expertly applied that Ciaran could not see a single brushstroke. He could, however, tell where some of the original paint had not been fully covered by the new. The paint made from the pigments Ciaran had returned with was purer, its color not fading like the other did as it dried. Ciaran wondered if he was just imagining things. Regardless, it was not the quality of the paint that made this a masterpiece. It was clear to Ciaran that Master Edgar had an expert eye for using color to create the illusion of life.

By midday, Master Edgar finished his painting. His final stroke of the brush was a signature rune placed in the bottom left corner. It was done with a vibrant red paint which contrasted with the yellow and green hillside which it was placed upon. Ciaran watched, curious, as Master Edgar took a single minute to admire his work before going about cleaning up his palate.

"Come boy, help me wash the brushes. Then you can go home. Tomorrow we will start building the frame. But nothing more can be done until everything dries."

"Of course."

Ciaran took the paint brushes and went out back where he scrubbed them clean with turpentine. The foul smelling stuff bothered Ciaran and he kept rubbing his nose on his shoulder. He cleaned the brushes three times before he was satisfied that he had removed the paint. Near the outdoor washing station was a table with many holes made in the surface. Placing the ends of the brushes in the holes, he left them upside down to dry. Drawing water from the backyard well, he washed the foul smelling turpentine from his hands, and then for good measure washed his face. Feeling just a bit more refreshed, Ciaran went back inside where he found Master Edgar working at one of his tables.

"The brushes have been washed and I've set them out to dry."

"Good lad. You've done well."

"Is there anything else you need from me before I go home?"

"Only for you to tell me what you have been working on."

"What do you mean?"

"Do not lie to me boy. I know you have been working on a painting. I've seen you sneak away paints every few days."

Ciaran stood, stunned, uncertain what to say.

"I am not angry with you. I didn't stop you for a reason. In fact, I would be angry if you were not working on something." Master Edgar turned around in his stool and gave Ciaran one of his familiar raised eyebrow stairs. "Tell me, what have you been working on?"

"It's a painting of the dragon who burned the temple."

Master Edgar didn't laugh or even grow angry. He simply gave Ciaran a nod, then turned his attention back to the table. "Why did you choose that as your subject?"

"The dragon is majestic. I can think of no better subject for my painting."

"I see. So you feel it then?"

"Feel what?"

"That inner longing that pushes you to create. The thing that tells you what to do if you are willing to listen to it. Like the Goddess herself has planted an idea in your mind that must be brought forth."

Ciaran paused, taking a moment to reflect and examine something he had never before considered. "I think I do understand what you are describing. And to answer your question, yes, I feel it."

"Then, Ciaran, I am even more proud that you have been my apprentice. I would very much like to see it."

"I'm not finished yet."

"Oh, then you better hurry home to do so. If you wait any longer, there won't be enough time for it to dry for the presentation at the temple."

"I had decided not to present it."

Master Edgar wheeled around. "And why not?"

Ciaran shrugged and then gestured to the large canvas Master Edgar had just finished. "I am no master painter. Besides, I don't think anyone would be happy to have an artwork of the dragon who ruined the temple."

"If that is your desire, I shall not force you, but I would strongly recommend it."

"Why?"

"Art has two purposes. The first is to give you, as an artist, the opportunity to express and bring to life all the innate creativity the Goddess has decided to bless you with. The second is to be seen, to plant the desire and wonder into the hearts of those who were meant to see it. Art that has been hidden away sadly missed that second opportunity and never fulfills its purpose."

"But what if the painting isn't good enough? What if there are mistakes?"

"What piece of art doesn't have a mistake?" Master Edgar stood up and shook his head. Though his voice had seemed stern, his face was split by a large smile. "There is no such thing as a perfect painting Ciaran."

"I would call that perfect," Ciaran argued, gesturing to the drying masterpiece.

"You have spent weeks watching me. How often did you

see me scrape away some color, blend out a color, or add another layer to change how something looked?"

"Every day."

"Were those not mistakes?"

"I thought that was how painting was done. That it took time and layers to create what you were hoping to make."

"That, my dear Ciaran, is exactly the point I am trying to make. You call them mistakes, they are not. It is simply how you put down the paint. Part of it is an accident, part of it is intentional. But then you work on it and turn every previous action into something meaningful."

"But in the end, you have created something that captures the reality and beauty of life. What if my painting doesn't?"

"Why would that bother you?"

Ciaran opened his mouth to speak, but couldn't find the words.

"Let us not argue this point any further. Go home now and finish your painting. Once it has been given time to dry, I would very much like you to bring it here. We can talk of this more at that time. I would like you to consider the idea that no matter how imperfect you think your painting is, that it is still worth presenting to the city at the festival."

"I will."

Without another word, Ciaran left the studio. His mind ran over and over the words that Master Edgar had spoken to him. He found that walking helped him think and when he reached his home he was filled with renewed excitement. When he walked inside he found his mother sitting in the rocking chair beside the fire, a piece of embroidery in her hands.

"You are home early," his mother said, glancing up from her needlework.

"Master Edgar finished his painting today. Said there was no more work to be done until tomorrow."

"Have you eaten?"

"Not yet."

"Well then, I will prepare something for you. Why don't you go upstairs and find Zict. It will be nice to have lunch together."

"I will go get him."

Ciaran went upstairs to his bedroom, his thoughts on painting and not food. When he entered his room, the smell of the paint was almost overwhelming. He found Zict, sitting on his bed, playing with a ball of string.

"What are you doing home so soon?" Zict said, setting down the string.

"Edgar is done with his painting. He sent me home so I can finish mine."

Ciaran looked at the painting in the corner. The soaring dragon was lacking the detail he truly wanted to make it great. All of the color was there, but the texture of the scales was missing. He wondered how he would be able to manage adding the rest of the fine details in a single evening.

"So, does this mean you are going to present it?"

"Now that I have told Master Edgar about it, I don't think he's going to leave me with the choice."

"Then we need to get to work."

"I don't think I am going to be able to do it, Zict."

"Nonsense. Just think, we have an entire afternoon to work. That is plenty of time."

"Are you sure?"

"Of course. Hurry, let's go and eat. I know you can do this. No matter what happens, I'm certain that Avot would be proud."

"Thanks Zict. Perhaps the next time we go to visit, we can show it to him."

"Or, perhaps he will surprise us all and visit us during the festival."

Ciaran barked a laugh and shook his head. "Wouldn't that be a surprise."

16
THE RED TUNIC

The day of the festival had finally arrived and Ciaran woke before dawn. He couldn't fall back asleep and stayed in bed until the first rays of sunlight broke through the gap in his window curtains. Pulling back his blankets, Ciaran almost leapt from his bed in excitement. Zict was still fast asleep in the small bed which he had created for himself. More of a hammock, the bed of knotted rope hung from a hook in the ceiling and served Zict like a nest. The goblin was not the least bit disturbed, curled up in a mess of handkerchiefs and a small rabbit pelt. Zict was snoring slightly, the sound like a lazy bumble bee bumping around flower petals.

Drawing back the curtains, Ciaran looked out at the brilliant yellow sun that was peeking up over the mountains. He longed for those peaks and the dragon's palace that lay beyond. Part of him still didn't feel as if it had returned. Like his heart would forever be there, calling back to him, and wishing for him to return. Smiling, Ciaran turned around and looked at the painting which he had set against the far wall. The image of Avot in flight against a cloudy blue sky and hazy mountains was something he was proud of. In the early morning sunlight, the red paint of the dragon's scales glowed while the black underbelly complemented the color with shadow. He walked over and placed his thumb against the bottom right corner of the canvas where he had signed the painting. The rune for his name was done with yellow, making it stand out from the cool blue color of the mountain foothill it covered. He had done his best to keep it small and he hoped that it wouldn't call too much attention. Taking one final look at the painting, Ciaran sighed, then went to his desk where he'd placed a folded up sheet of old linen.

Using the old sheet to wrap the canvas, he placed the painting on his bed, then began to get ready for the day. Zict was still fast asleep in his nest and Ciaran didn't hear movements downstairs. He sat down beside his painting, then decided to forgo breakfast and hurry to Master Edgar's studio. Eager to show his master the painting and fit it into the frame, Ciaran put on his shoes and then quietly crept from his house.

The morning was still cool but he could feel the ending of spring. Breathing deeply, he took in the clean scent of fresh dew that clung to the homes and plants that grew between them. Striding up the cobblestones, he found that the movement brought a bit of warmth back into him.

Though much of the city was still asleep, there were

enough people out and about their business that Ciaran found himself politely greeting someone every few minutes. He didn't mind and almost everyone gave him a bit larger of a smile than usual. It took him a while before realizing that the enthusiasm was a result of the covered painting he carried. That had gained him respect, even though none of them could see what he had made.

When he reached the main road, Ciaran found that the market was already being set up. People rushed about hanging tarps and setting up booths. Members of the city guard were also walking about, directing people and providing some degree of organization. He moved a bit slower as he walked through the market, making sure he didn't accidentally bump into anyone, or worse, that someone didn't accidentally bump into his canvas. It was an immediate relief when he reached the far end of the market and was no longer amidst the bustling people. Ciaran had a feeling that it was going to be a long busy day.

When he reached the artisan street, there were even more people about, most of them dressed in green tunics. Ciaran walked by them and was, for the most part, ignored. They had learned of him over the last few weeks and he had not gained favorable rapport with any of them. Ciaran had learned to ignore the dirty looks they gave him, but he felt self conscious this morning. His heart began to beat just a little faster in his chest. Several of them gave him second glances as he walked past, their attention drawn to the wrapped canvas he held.

"What you got there?" a familiar voice said from behind.

Ciaran paused, then looked over his shoulder. He recognized Declan who was walking up the street with seven other apprentices. Five were boys and two were girls, all about the same age. Their tunics were a bit nicer today, the green more vibrant, their leather belts shining. Several of them all had golden rings on their fingers and the girls had golden chains woven into their hair. Declan smiled wider as the group approached. He had a strange gleam in his eye and Ciaran wondered if they were excited for the festival.

"You gonna' answer the question, or just stand there like an idiot?" one of the other boys asked.

"It's a painting."

"Well that's obvious," one of the girls said. "Who'd you steal it from?"

"I didn't steal it from anyone. It's mine."

They started to laugh at him. Ciaran took a step back and scowled. This only made the group of older kids laugh louder.

"Oh, leave him alone," Declan said. He walked forward and placed his hand on Ciaran's shoulder. "He's probably wrapped it all up because he's ashamed of it."

Ciaran pulled away and then began to stock away. Two of the apprentices from the group rushed forward and blocked his way forward. When Ciaran tried to get around them, one of the girls bounded forward and grabbed the edge of the painting. Before he could adjust his own grip, the painting was pulled out of his hands.

"Give it back!" Ciaran demanded.

The girl just laughed, dancing back. Declan jeered at

him and the two other apprentices who had been blocking his way took hold of Ciaran's shoulders. He tried and failed to pull away from the boys who were holding him.

"Show us the painting, Fiona," Declan said.

Fiona, the girl who had taken the painting, began to unwrap the linen sheet. She let it fall to the ground and then started to laugh. She turned the painting around and showed it to everyone. She swayed back and forth so everyone could see. A few more of the apprentices had come to see what was going on. Ciaran heard a few jeers, a slew of insults, and a curse or two.

"What is this? Some sort of joke." Declan strode forward and yanked the canvas out of Fiona's hands. "No wonder you wanted to keep this covered. What a waste of perfectly good paint and canvas."

Several of the other boys went over to Declan and one of them, who had a pointed nose and small ears, whispered something into his ear.

"Great idea, Cormac, you're right. Let's trash it."

Ciaran opened his mouth to scream, cry out for help, but no sound came. His heart wrenched when the boys took both sides of his painting and twisted. The wooden frame groaned and cracked. As the frame broke, the canvas went loose and they continued to pull. The paint began to stretch and warp. Several large cracks formed. Once the painting was mangled, they threw it onto the ground and began to grind it into the cobblestones with their heels. Laughter and cheering sounded from the boys that held him.

A firm voice shouted over the commotion and the laughter stopped.

"Lord Aidan," a voice in the crowd whispered.

The boys who had been holding Ciaran let him go. As they ran away, Ciaran sank to his knees. He looked at his mangled painting and tears welled in his eyes. As his throat tightened and vision blurred, he fought for control over his emotions. He did not want to cry in the street in front of the others. Ciaran just wanted time to stop.

A hand gently gripped his shoulder and Ciaran whirled around, growling. The man who stood above him was dressed in fine red clothing and a black cape. Lord Aidan's hair was slicked back with oil and he smelled of rich perfumes. A grave look was on the master artisans face as he looked from Ciaran to the painting.

"Get to your feet boy," Lord Aidan said, his voice kinder than expected.

Ciaran pulled away, crawled over to his painting, then taking hold of the sides of the canvas, lifted it off the ground. When he turned it over, he saw that the stones had worn away large sections of the paint and all of the detail of the dragon's face was gone. Clutching his painting to his chest, Ciaran stood, then started to walk away. To both his irritation and relief, Lord Aidan followed.

The apprentices had all but disappeared from the street, though Ciaran could see that several were looking at him from nearby windows. His eyes still stung with tears, but he took slow deliberate breaths, keeping himself calm enough so that they wouldn't fall. When he reached the bakery at the end, he saw a crate set outside. Walking over to it, Ciaran collapsed upon it. Unable to keep his emotions at bay any longer, Ciaran started to cry.

Hot tears spilled down his face, collecting at his chin and dripping down onto the ruined painting. Ciaran made little noise, though he wanted to shout and scream. Instead, he just allowed himself to feel sorry about his loss. He knew there was nothing more that could be done. Time didn't seem to matter all that much and Ciaran remained wholly unaware of everything else that was going on around him. When the tears stopped falling, he wiped his eyes with his sleeve, then looked up. Lord Aidan was still standing there, a grim expression on his face.

Ciaran looked at the man, uncertain why he was still there. At first, he felt the need to bow, but his anger was still fresh enough that he was able to set aside the need to honor someone so much higher than his own station. Ciaran just wanted to be left alone.

"What do you want?" Ciaran asked, his voice cracking.

"Are you alright?"

"I will be. I just want to be left alone."

"Where are you off to?"

Ciaran gestured over his shoulder with his thumb.

"You are Master Edgar's student?"

"I was."

"Not any longer."

"I am."

"Let us go to him then."

"You don't need to follow me. There isn't anything you can do to fix this."

"I know; and for that I am truly sorry."

"Then go, leave me here. I don't need to be accompanied by anyone. There isn't anything left that I need to protect."

"All the same, I would still like to visit my old master with you anyway."

Seeing that he wouldn't be able to get rid of the man, Ciaran forced himself to his feet, then started walking down the street towards Edgar's studio. His anger was replaced by an overwhelming desire to return home and go to bed. He didn't want to think, he didn't want to feel. Ciaran just wanted the day to be over.

When they reached the red door to Edgar's studio, Lord Aidan knocked. Ciaran held the remnants of his painting close to his chest, his eyes downcast. He was having a hard time focusing. The sound of the door opening drew Ciaran's attention and when he looked up, he saw that his teacher was dressed in fine red robes. They were of an older style, but they made him look regal as a king. His hair had been trimmed short and his face shaved clean. For the first time since Ciaran had seen Edgar, he looked like the master artisan he was. The smile Edgar wore faded the moment his eyes fell upon Ciaran. Then, his brow furrowed and he snarled, turning his attention to Lord Aidan.

"What have you done to my student?" Edgar demanded.

"To my shame, I was able to do nothing. The other apprentices set upon your student and were in the middle of harassing him when I intervened. But it was too late, for they had already destroyed his painting."

Ciaran felt a sharp pain in his heart and he clutched the ruined canvas even closer. He wanted to find a hole and hide himself forever.

"My dear boy," Edgar said, walking out and placing an arm around Ciaran. "Come inside, let us see if something can be done."

"It's too late," Ciaran whispered.

Edgar said nothing more. Instead, he helped Ciaran into the studio. Ciaran wasn't really thinking and he just went through the motions, his mind so far away. The thoughts of finding a hole to hide in faded, but he still wanted escape. He no longer wished to be in Umrithos and instead longed to be back at Avot's palace. There he would feel safe. There he would not have to worry about his paintings being destroyed.

When they entered the studio, the three of them went to a table and Ciaran set down his painting. Taking a step back, he let Edgar and Aidan examine it. Not wanting to see his ruined work, Ciaran walked away and then stopped in front of Master Edgar's painting. Now set in a golden frame, the painting of Umrithos was beautiful. It was so much better than his own work had been. Now that his efforts had been for naught, Ciaran realized how foolish they had been in the first place. He should not have tried to paint. All of the pain and anger that had welled up inside of him vanished and he collapsed, completely exhausted, on a nearby stool. Though his master started to speak, Ciaran didn't hear any of the words. He continued to look at the ground, empty of both thought and feeling.

"You should be proud of yourself," Master Edgar said, his voice finally breaking through Ciaran's mental fog.

He turned around and saw that Edgar was standing alone at the table. Ciaran looked around and saw that Aidan was gone.

"Why?"

"The work you have done, Ciaran, is remarkable. Your use of color is near mastery."

"But the brushwork is not refined. The details are lacking in clarity."

"Ogres bath water!" Edgar said, waving his hand. "Details come in time. You don't realize how difficult it is to not muddy colors when painting, do you?"

"It's just color."

"Just color?" Edgar shook his head and let out a laugh. "Just color. Boy, I wish I had a fraction of your ability to see."

"If you are trying to make me feel better, please don't."

"Don't mistake my praise for a desire to lift your spirits. If this tragedy had ever happened to my work, I might have given up and died on the spot." Edgar's smile turned into a frown and the wrinkles between his eyebrows and the creases on his forehead deepened. "But do not give up. Do not let this keep you from painting again."

Ciaran knew that the words were meant to uplift him,

to make him feel encouraged. Instead, they just made him feel more hollow.

"I won't give up," Ciaran lied so the encouragement would end. "Is there anything you need from me today?"

"There isn't much for you to do. The priestess and the royal family have prepared waggons to take our paintings to the temple for the festival. They will be by this morning and should be able to help get the painting where it needs to go."

"Can I go home then?"

"You can. But wait here for just a moment longer. Aidan went to get something for you. Once he returns, you will be free to do as you wish."

"I will wait then."

"Would you like sweet rolls and cream?" Edgar asked.

Ciaran's stomach rumbled at the mention of food, and he nodded. Edgar left the main room of the studio, then returned with a plate filled with the sweet rolls. He gave the plate to Ciaran who examined the cream covered pastries. Each of the rolls were small and plucking one out with his fingers, he shoved the entire thing into his mouth. The pastry was soft, warm, and sweet as sugar. It made him feel a touch better and with almost ravenous hunger, he devoured the entire plate. Licking the sticky cream from off his fingers, Ciaran thanked Edgar who was slowly eating from his own plate.

Leaving the empty plate on the table, Ciaran went out to the back to draw water from the well. He wanted to get a drink and wash up a bit. Drawing half a bucket, he drank first, washing down the sweet rolls with frigid water. Then, he cleaned his hands and face. It felt good to wash away the dried tears from his cheeks. Cleaning a bit of crusty residue from the corners of his eyes, he dumped the rest of the water onto the large tree that grew in the corner, then replaced the bucket. When he went back inside, he saw that Lord Aidan had returned and was holding a wrapped bundle under his arm.

"Ciaran," Lord Aidan said, becoming him over. "I have something for you."

Joining Aidan and Edgar by the tables, he couldn't help but feel wary as he examined the package. Aidan handed Ciaran the package which was soft and light. Ciaran hesitated for only a moment, then removed the string and paper. Inside was a new red tunic. The fabric was soft and rich. Ciaran looked up and saw that the two artists were smiling at him.

"Why are you giving me this? I thought I was supposed to be wearing green."

"Only an apprentice wears green," Master Edgar said. "We no longer felt it was appropriate for you to work under that title."

"In our assessment, you have, even in the short time working under the tutelage and direction of High Master Edgar, reached sufficient understanding of the techniques of painting that you have been accepted as the newest junior member of the artisans guild." Lord Aidan reached into his pocket and produced a simple silver ring. He held it out to Ciaran and continued, "you may pursue any professional commission and have an official place in our guild. All accommodations, resources, and accreditations are yours."

Ciaran took the silver signet ring and examined the flat surface where the symbol of the artisan's guild had been engraved. Though he was astonished at the sudden elevation in his status, Ciaran didn't put on the ring. Instead, he looked up at Edgar and Aidan who were both smiling at him.

"Isn't this supposed to be more official?"

"It will be. You shall be presented at the festival with the other newly elevated artists. Though we were only expecting to elevate three from apprentice to junior artisan, adding a fourth will be of little consequence."

"I am honored, but I don't think I can accept."

Ciaran made to hand the ring back, but Aidan shook his head.

"The offer has been extended. If you do not want to accept, than you must choose not to present yourself today."

"If you are just doing this to make me feel better, I don't want your pity."

"Ciaran," Edgar said, his voice unusually gentle. "We are not doing this out of pity. You deserve a place in the guild. It is the best place for you to continue growing your abilities."

"But I have only been an apprentice for a few short months. There are others who have been doing this for years. How is it fair that I should be admitted as a junior guild member in such a short time?"

Lord Aidan smiled, "you see things very well Ciaran, but you are missing something. One can spend years learning at the feet of masters, having their every mistake corrected until they produce work that is the same as the person teaching them. Eventually, reaching a point where higher learning must be achieved through your own experience. Just because you are an official member doesn't mean you are a master. But, you now have the status to work as you will and learn by completing your own commissions rather than by assisting another with theirs. It will be through doing, rather than helping, that you continue to learn"

Ciaran looked back down at the silver signet ring, then placed it on his right middle finger. It fit well and he felt a sense of confidence fill him. After a few moments of silence, he looked back at the masters and muttered a simple thanks.

"I'm going to return home, but I will be there for the presentation."

"Good lad," Master Edgar said. "We'll be waiting for you."

Departing, Ciaran left the two masters behind. When he stepped out onto the street, he looked up at the sky and noticed the clouds which were drifting in from the horizon. A chill wind had started and the shift in weather almost made him feel like it was a new start to the day. He kept the package tucked under his arm as he went. A few apprentices were back out on the street and everyone gave him a wide berth. He didn't bother looking at any of them or at anyone who might be watching from the windows. He just continued on his way, an even mix of hope and melancholy swirling around in his chest. All he could do was keep moving forward, no matter what.

17
THE FESTIVAL

Dressed in his new red tunic, black trousers, and red cape, Ciaran couldn't help but feel a bit strange. Standing alone in his kitchen, he looked out the window at the people hurrying through the street. His parents still hadn't returned from the market and Ciaran was getting tired of waiting around. Not wanting to leave and go to the temple grounds without them, he found solace in pacing back and forth.

Zict was sitting on the kitchen table, tapping his fingers on the wood.

"Do you want to go for a walk outside?" the goblin suggested. "It might be better than walking around the kitchen."

"It's too busy outside for a good walk. Besides, I don't want to get caught up in something and arrive late."

"Well, why don't you do some drawing."

"I'm not really in the mood, Zict. I could just as easily

lose track of time doing that as well. I really don't want to be late."

His friend nodded and didn't press the issue. The goblin had said little about the ruined painting. Compared to the sympathy he'd received from his parents, it was a welcome relief that Zict seemed to share in his sorrow.

A knock sounded at the door and a wave of relief coursed through him. Rushing to the door, Ciaran opened it and saw Maeve standing on his front step. Her red hair was done up in a braid that spiraled around the back of her head and was held secure with two glass needles. He saw that green glass butterflies had been added to the ends of the needles which accented the look perfectly. Her dress was also a vibrant green, like the fresh growths of pine needles and she was wearing gloves which went to her elbows.

"Wow," Maeve said, "where did you get such nice clothes?"

"They were a gift."

"Are they supposed to be red?"

Ciaran held out his hand and showed her the signet ring.

"You're joking with me!" Maeve said with a big smile.

Ciaran shook his head. "It's no joke. I am going to be made an official member of the guild today."

"Congratulations. I'm so happy for you." Maeve bounded in and gave him a hug. "So, did they love the painting?"

Ciaran broke away from the hug and sighed. "I suppose in a way, they liked it."

"What does that mean?"

"It got ruined while I was on my way to Edgar's studio."

"Oh Ciaran, I'm so sorry. How did it happen?"

"A few of the other apprentices got a hold of it. I don't really want to talk about it."

"So, you won't have anything to present at the festival?"

"No."

"What about your other paintings?"

"I did those before. I don't want to present any of them."

Maeve smiled wide and bounced up on her toes. "I know. Why don't you present your sketchbook?"

"I don't know."

"That's a wonderful idea, Maeve," Zict said from the table. He leaped onto Ciaran's shoulder, his wide smile splitting his face from ear to ear.

"Nice to see you, Zict."

"You as well, Maeve."

"I don't feel like presenting anything. But I appreciate the enthusiasm."

"And why not?" Maeve demanded.

Ciaran shrugged. "It doesn't make sense to present a sketchbook."

"Why not?"

"The other artists won't find it all that impressive. It's just a bunch of my own drawings and simple paintings."

"But they are beautiful," Maeve said. "And you aren't presenting it to them. Isn't the point to present it to Umris?"

Nodding, Ciaran felt foolish. "You are right. As usual."

"Ciaran doesn't win a lot of arguments," Zict said.

Maeve laughed. "That's not the point of arguing, Zict."

"Is too," the goblin said, bounding from Ciaran's shoulder to hers.

"I think you just like to argue."

"Not true," Zict said. "It's just a common necessity to help people understand that I'm right."

Leaving his friends to continue their banter, Ciaran went upstairs to his bedroom. He found his sketchbook on his desk and picking it up, he undid the leather strap which held the book closed. Taking a moment, he glanced through the pages, looking once more at all the drawings and paintings. Fondness filled him as memories of his journey came back in vivid detail. Smiling to himself, Ciaran turned to the last page where he had drawn Avot. Muttering thanks to the dragon, Ciaran closed the book and left his bedroom. He was grateful for the dragon and the fire that had started this whole journey. Remembering the other paintings that had burned, Ciaran felt the weight of his loss reduced. With a bit more spring to his step, Ciaran went back downstairs and joined his friends. Zict was in the middle of some strange story about a frog and a weasel fighting over a snake's egg. It didn't make much sense, but the goblin's enthusiastic mannerisms made Ciaran smile. They laughed together as Zict told his story and Ciaran found that the jovial atmosphere relieved most tension he'd been carrying in his shoulders. When Ciaran's parents returned from the market, Zict hid himself in Ciaran's pocket, and they left for the temple.

Ciaran felt uncomfortable as he sat beside Master Edgar. Their chairs were placed on the edge of a large wooden stage that had been built on the right side of the temple. They were joined by all the other artisans and master painters. Lord Aidan sat in the very front just to the right of the King and Queen. All of the apprentices were sitting on a row of benches that had been set up on the side of the stage. Ciaran glanced their way once or twice and each time he saw looks of astonishment on their faces. He didn't seek out Declan or any of the others who had ruined his painting that morning. Instead, he ignored them and tried to keep calm. With every passing minute, his heart seemed to beat even faster until it was thumping like a jackrabbit in his chest.

There was a gap in front of the stage that was a hundred spans long. After the gap, more than a hundred large benches had been set out, forming neat rows on the grassy temple grounds. These were filled with the more wealthy aristocratic families, minor royalty, merchants, and bankers. The rest of the people were left to stand. Ciaran saw his parents standing with Maeve and her parents behind the last row of benches. They were smiling at him.

He remained sitting in silence for an hour. A few more people arrived, and the noise from the chatter was almost overwhelming. The priestess stood, walked to the front of the stage, and stepped up onto the raised platform in the center. She wore brilliant white robes and her arms were covered in golden bracelets. The chattering crowd went silent as she raised her hand.

"Welcome all! In celebration of the goodness of the season and of our patron Goddess Umris, we will commence our celebration with the presentation of new artisans."

Edgar grumbled and prodded Ciaran with his elbow.

His heart began to race and Ciaran stood. Three more people got to their feet, a boy and two girls who were several years Ciaran's senior. The four of them joined the priestess at the front of the stage and Ciaran put on his best smile.

"Raise up your right hands," the priestess instructed.

Ciaran raised his hand, his signet ring shining in the sunlight.

Cheers erupted from the crowd and then the other three bowed. Following their lead, Ciaran felt his ears grow hot. He felt unprepared for this and wanted to return to his seat. The other artists straightened up and took a unified step back. Ciaran joined them, trying his best not to feel embarrassed.

"Before you stand four remarkable artists who have been deemed worthy of their masters to become junior artisans. We would like you all to join in a round of applause to congratulate them on their diligent efforts."

The crowd applauded and Ciaran felt his cheeks grow red.

"Thank you," the priestess said.

She turned towards them and one by one, shook their

hands. She gave Ciaran a big smile when she shook his hand and he smiled back. When this was done, they received another round of applause. To his relief, the others started towards their seats and Ciaran eagerly went to his own. Once he was seated, he turned his attention back to the priestess.

"Now we are all still filled with sorrow at the loss of the many great paintings that were burned in the fire. For three months, all of our wonderful painters have been hard at work preparing new masterpieces. Without any further delay, let us begin the presentation of art."

Lord Aidan was the first to stand and with a wave of his hand, several boys in green carried his painting onto the stage. It was draped with a red cloth. Once it was set on a stand, Lord Aidan pulled off the cloth and revealed his painting. The crowd gasped and then clapping ensued. Ciaran was left breathless as he looked at the painting. The master painter had perfectly recreated the original painting of Umris that had hung as the centerpiece of the temple before its burning. Ciaran smiled, thinking of the other version of the painting that hung in Avot's palace. At that moment, Ciaran knew that Lord Aidan had already won the contest. It almost seemed a shame that Aidan had been allowed to present his first.

Ciaran felt a sense of relief come over him. He reached down and picked up his sketchbook, the leather cover feeling soft in his hands. Ciaran was happy to let the others present their paintings. He no longer felt any need to be compared to them. The pressure he'd felt had abated and it no longer seemed important that what he was going to present wasn't a masterwork.

For the next hour, artists presented their paintings in the order that they were seated on the stage. When one of the other artists who had also been presented got up to present a painting, Ciaran realized that he would be the last person to present. He had to keep himself from laughing. He found humor in speculating how everyone else would react. Though he managed to remain calm for another hour, his heart began to race when Master Edgar got up to present his painting. The clapping was almost as loud in response to the reveal of Edgar's painting as it had been for the one Lord Aidan presented. Suddenly, the pressure of having to present returned and Ciaran's hands began to tremble.

Don't worry about what anyone else thinks, he told himself.

When Master Edgar returned to his seat, Ciaran took a deep breath, then stood. He glanced at Maeve who smiled and waved to him. He smiled back and then felt Zict move in his pocket. He glanced down and saw the tip of his friend's ear poke out. He reached down and gave it a gentle tap. Zict shifted, once again concealing himself within Ciaran's pocket.

The priestess greeted him and he held out his sketchbook.

"A simple gift for the Goddess," Ciaran said. He then bowed to the priestess. She took the sketchbook and he stood up straight once more. "My sincerest thanks to her and the gift of art she has shared with our city."

Smiling, the priestess, held up the journal for all to see. No one clapped in response to his gift. Instead people began to murmur. Ciaran didn't feel embarrassment or shame. Instead, he felt a profound calmness enter his heart.

"You may return to your seat."

Walking in front of the stage, Ciaran met Lord Aidan's eye and the master artist gave him a nod of approval. He was the only one. Everyone else just gave him strange looks that ranged from amusement to disbelief. Glancing at the apprentices, he smiled at them and ignored their bewildered expressions. He realized that Declan and the others who had helped to destroy his painting were not among them. He almost wished that they had been there to see him. Sitting back down, Master Edgar leaned over and chuckled.

"That was interesting. You should prepare yourself for the gossip. You may have just created an interesting reputation for yourself."

"The gift wasn't for them," Ciaran said, glancing at the crowd. "I think there were enough beautiful paintings presented that the temple will once again be a place of astonishing beauty."

"You know you didn't have to present anything."

"I figured as much."

"I'm glad you did."

"Thank you."

Several people stood which drew Ciaran's attention. The King and Queen joined the priestess at the front of the stage. The raised platform was just large enough for the three of them to stand together. In unison, they started the song which would begin the more traditional part of the festival celebration. Everyone remained quiet for the first verse, then joined in on the second. Cheers erupted at the end of the song and music began to play from drums, harps, and lutes. The festival had officially begun and Ciaran left the other artists so he could enjoy the celebrations with his family.

☙ 18 ❧
THE STRANGE VISITOR

The sun was setting and Ciaran found himself standing alone on the edge of the temple grounds. Built atop the highest hill of the city, Ciaran had a perfect view of Umrithos. His attention didn't linger long on the city, instead focusing on the distant mountains where he watched the sun descend and touch the tips of the distant peaks. Large clouds covered the sky and were ablaze with the colors of the dying day. It was like a brush had been swept across the sky, leaving behind highlights of pink and yellow atop purple and blue clouds. Where he could see the sky beyond, he saw nothing but brilliant oranges. He was awestruck by the beauty and glad to have made his escape from the crowd to enjoy it. Ciaran knew that the moments of color wouldn't last long and he tried to savor the moment. Zict had crawled from his pocket and was perched atop his shoulder.

"Now that is something you should paint," Zict said.

"Without a doubt. It shall be my next project."

"Are you still sad?"

"Not really. I'm actually very happy right now."

"Good. Who knows, you might find that the next time you try to paint Avot, it will turn out even better."

"I am certain of that."

"Have you thought about going for another journey?" Zict asked.

"The thought has crossed my mind. There should be enough paint left for a few more projects. I'd like to complete my first commission before I go out again. I suspect that by the end of summer, I will be ready to go on another journey."

"I think it would be a joy to discover some new colors and pigments," Zict said. "Perhaps we might even meet new creatures along the way."

"That would be wonderful. Do you already have a few places in mind?"

"I do."

They were silent again and the sky was continuing to change, the colors fading into darker orange and purple hughes.

"What about you, Zict? Are you happy?"

"More than I think I have ever been."

"I didn't expect you to enjoy being around so many humans."

"You aren't all that bad. Besides, it has been fun to watch you work. I hope to do even more of it."

"Zict, you are always welcome to come watch me work

when I take commissions. You don't have to stay in my room all of the time. I bet Master Edgar wouldn't mind if you wanted to watch him as well."

"I'm not ready to be introduced to anyone else yet," Zict said. "But soon enough I expect to have a red tunic of my own."

"And a little silver ring," Ciaran added.

"Yes, and my own silver ring."

The sound of footsteps behind them made Zict's ears twitch and he climbed down Ciaran's tunic and disappeared into his pocket. A moment later, the priestess joined him on the side of the hill. Now that she wasn't standing on a platform, Ciaran realized that she wasn't actually taller than him. Instead, they were the same height.

"Mind if I join you."

"Of course not," Ciaran said, bowing his head. "I would be glad for the company."

"Aidan told me what happened to you this morning. I am deeply sorry."

"Thank you, but there is no longer any need to be sorry. Just as there is no need to be sorry that the other paintings were burned."

"Are you certain that is how you feel?"

"I am. It is obvious to me now. A friend prepared me for this, though I don't think that was his intention."

"I see. Then, why do you stand here alone while the others celebrate?"

"I came here to enjoy the colors of the sunset. No matter how long we live, there will never be another just like it. It seemed like a shame for no one to take a moment to enjoy it while it was here to be appreciated."

The priestess nodded, and they watched the sunset until the last bits of orange faded to deep purple and blue. When the sunset was over, and night had begun, Ciaran looked back at the priestess. She met his eyes and motioned towards the temple.

"Come with me," the priestess said, turning around.

Ciaran followed her, making their way from the edge of the hill to the temple. When they reached the crowd of other artists in red, they parted for them. Most held goblets in their hands and were laughing as they conversed with one another. The music continued to play and for a moment seemed unbearably loud when they strode directly in front of the drummers. The vibrations from the percussion made Ciaran's body vibrate. It was a relief when they passed them by and exited the crowd of people. The priestess led him to the front of the temple and up the steps.

Through the open doors, he could see that all of the new paintings had been hung on the walls. As expected, Lord Aidan's painting had been placed on the far wall in place of the one which had been burned. He remembered the way the marble had been scorched black and was relieved to find that it was now as white and brilliant as it had ever been. Glancing up at the rafters, he saw that the new wooden roof was even more exquisite. Each beam had been worked with chisels and tools in a way that made them look like natural branches of a tree. Ciaran was reminded of the dark forest canopy he had traveled through. He smiled.

"It's beautiful," Ciaran said. "I am glad to see so much has been restored. Thank you for bringing me here to show it to me."

"I am glad you enjoy the new display, but that is not why I brought you here."

"Why then?"

"You will see. Just keep following me."

The priestess continued on, walking swiftly down the large main room of the temple. She led them to the back corner and opened the gate to a stairwell. She glanced back at him, then began to ascend to the second story. Ciaran felt excitement course through him. He'd never been up to the second story of the temple before and was suddenly anxious to know what he would see.

When they reached the top, Ciaran found himself in a room as long as the one below, but with a ceiling that was only ten feet in height rather than fifty. The ceiling was angled and the underside was carved with hundreds of wooden leaves. On the opposite side of the room Ciaran saw a balcony. The priestess was walking towards it.

As he followed her, Ciaran looked at the stone pedestals which lined the walls. Each of them had a smooth white tip and different objects had been placed upon them. Ciaran couldn't help but stop to look at them as they passed. He saw a paint brush, a bottle of paints, a simple painting of a woman's face in a wooden frame, pieces of painted pottery, and other small works of art that ranged from jewelry to woven baskets. Each of the objects were so different from the large masterpieces on display in the room below. At the end, Ciaran saw his own sketchbook set out on a stone pedestal. It had been left open, the drawing he had made of Avot on display. The priestess stopped before it and placed her fingers on the page.

"Why is this here?" Ciaran asked.

"Because it was my favorite piece presented today."

"It's only a sketchbook."

"Only a sketchbook?"

"I mean, it's not all that impressive."

"If you thought that, then why did you present it?"

"I just wanted to give it as a gift to Umris as a way to thank her. I knew that there would be other masterpieces presented today. But that sketchbook represents me in a way a simple painting never would. Since I no longer had a painting to present, my friends encouraged me to give Umris the one thing I had left. I am very surprised to hear that it was your favorite."

"I'm not the only one. There was another who also thought this was their favorite."

The priestess turned around and looked at the balcony. Ciaran followed her gaze and saw two people standing there. One figure he recognized as Avot. The dragon's red skin had an almost cold look in the moonlight. His golden eyes were fixated on Ciaran and Avot was smiling wide. The woman standing beside him had long golden hair and a white gown. She looked a great deal like the woman depicted in Lord Aidan's painting. Her golden hair shimmered like sunlight and her dark eyes examined him.

"Zict, you can come out," Avot said.

The goblin emerged from Ciaran's pocket and then crawled up to his shoulder.

"You did come!" Zict exclaimed. "I suspected you would."

Ciaran was too stunned to speak. He wasn't sure what to say.

"Thank you for your gift, Ciaran," Umris said. "I am proud to have it on display here as a reminder of why I chose to be the patron of this city."

Ciaran bowed deeply and when he stood up, he pulled his shoulders back and felt a great sense of pride.

"Never stop learning," the Goddess said. "I look forward to seeing you again."

Then, in a flash of golden light, Umris was gone, leaving Avot standing alone on the balcony. Ciaran looked from the dragon to the priestess and back again. The dragon smiled at him, then turned around and placed his large hands on the balcony. Ciaran and the priestess joined him. Zict bounded from Ciaran's shoulder and landed on Avot's. Looking out over the city, Ciaran saw that the streets were glowing from freshly lit paper lanterns. After a moment, the lanterns began to float towards the sky, like orange bubbles.

"Avot, may I ask you something?"

"Of course Ciaran."

"Next year, when we are preparing for the festival, I would like to try and do another painting of you. I was hoping you could pose for me. Would you allow that?"

"It would be my pleasure."

"Good. You deserve to have a painting done of you. A proper one and not just one done from my memory alone."

"I look forward to it."

"Help me understand something. Why did my art matter so much to the Goddess?"

"It's not that it mattered so much to her, but that she recognized how much it mattered to you. All the other pieces were done by artists looking to please others. Your book was done for you. And that made all the difference."

THE END

AFTERWORD

Thank you for reading, *The Wonder of Painting Dragons.* I hope that you enjoyed reading it as much as I enjoyed writing it. Creating this book and telling Ciaran's story was a deeply rewarding experience. But now this book and the story belongs to you, the reader. If you would like to leave a review to share your thoughts, I would greatly appreciate it. I know that this isn't a typical story, and I want to make sure it finds its way into the hands of the readers who will enjoy it. I truly appreciate all those who take the time to read my work, and I hope that this book brings both joy and wonder into your life.

Of all the stories I have told and the books I have written, this book was by far the most fun to work on. I wrote this story from a deeply personal place, examining my own heart and struggles with art in the process. For those who might be interested, I figured I would share the story behind the story. The idea for *The Wonder of Painting Dragons* came to me by accident. It was one of those rare moments when a few simple ideas struck me like lightning. Here is how it happened.

The first idea came to me while reading about Leonardo da Vinci's early life. I was fascinated by the description of Leonardo as a young artist, and that is when the first inkling of this story came into being. It was the faintest glimmer of a story about a young artist who wanted to pursue painting...dragons. I have always loved fantasy stories, so of course, my brain would immediately want to put this young painter protagonist in a fantastic setting filled with magic and monsters. But unlike much of my other work, this idea was simple and intended for a younger audience. As well, this idea appealed to my inner creativity. At first, I dismissed the idea of a story about a painter who lived in a fantasy world. Just because I had an idea for a character didn't mean I had enough for a full story. So, as many writers do, I set the idea on the back burner, hoping I could return to it soon.

A day later, I had the silly thought of what it would be like to have a goblin living on my shoulder whose sole purpose is to give me helpful advice. The concept made me laugh, and something in my brain made a connection. What if my young painter protagonist had such a goblin? One who specialized in art and provided my main character with mostly helpful advice as he tried to learn how to become the artist he dreamed of being. Suddenly, I had something that was bridging the gap between idea and story.

Soon after, the rest of the ideas for this story came

crashing down, and almost the entire plot outline was written in a single afternoon. This is the first time I have ever plotted a novel so quickly from start to finish. Everything fell into place, and with stunned amazement at the sheer luck of it all, I knew this book needed to be written. So, doing what any disciplined writer should do, I abandoned everything else I was working on to chase the shiny new story.

It was the idea for the art goblin that sold the idea for me. It was the comical yet relatable part that I felt a story of this nature needed. It wasn't until after I started writing the story that I realized why he was so important. I realized that I had my own internal art goblin.

Anyone who has tried to pursue a creative endeavor might be able to relate. You might also have your own little art goblin on your shoulder. To explain what I mean, I want to first address the idea of a muse. In Greek and Roman mythology, the daughters of Zeus were thought of as inspirations for the arts. Many writers, painters, dancers, and artists of all kinds have experience with the muses. That being said, the goblin is different from the muse. While the muse may serve as the source of inspiration for an artist and help influence his or her artistic expression, this is not the same function the goblin serves. The goblin is the ever-nagging voice that compels us to make art, even when we are not inspired. For me, if I do not write every day, a small voice within nags me to get to work. I often hear his voice scold me for not working on my art if I am putting it off. Only until I have done the work is the goblin satisfied and gives me a moment of peace.

Don't get me wrong. My goblin doesn't just nag. He also gives me the encouragement I need to seek out the adventure of creating. He's the one who tells me I have what it takes, so long as I am willing to try. The goblin gives me the courage to seek out the muse and to keep going even when I feel lost in the dark woods of creativity.

I hope that in some small way, I was able to capture that feeling in this story. This feeling served as the inspiration for the character Zict, who will forever have a place in my heart. No matter what type of artist you are, I would encourage you to keep going. Let your creativity make you and others happy.

ABOUT THE AUTHOR

Austin Colton is a jack of all trades who compulsively takes on far too many projects at once. He has found this a good strategy for curing perpetual boredom and a head stuck in the clouds. Austin lives in Arizona where he writes, paints, explores the great outdoors, and looks for new stories to enjoy. You can view his complete list of works and contact him online at:

AustinColton.com